THE STANFORD SISTERS

"I Didn't...I Never...Meant To Lead You On,"

Paige told Stefan.

"Lead me on?"

"Lead you on means to tease you." She swallowed. "To make you think I was inviting a chance to sleep with you...."

That, he had no trouble understanding. "We neck, yes. But we did not get it on. We did not hit your sack. You still even have your socks on. No reason to be afraid, Paige."

"I'm not afraid," she said sharply.

She was disastrous at fibbing, Stefan noted. She'd come apart in his arms as if she were a lover born for him. That kinship of spirits was rare and precious, and he couldn't believe he had mistaken her response.

And she was afraid. Of something.

Somehow Stefan had to find a way to uncover whatever it was.

Dear Reader,

It's the **CELEBRATION 1000** moment you've all been waiting for, the publication of Silhouette Desire #1000! As promised, it's a very special MAN OF THE MONTH by Diana Palmer called *Man of Ice*. Diana was one of the very first Silhouette Desire writers, and her many wonderful contributions to the line have made her one of our most beloved authors. This story is sure to make its way to your shelf of "keepers."

But that's not all! Don't miss *Baby Dreams,* the first book in a wonderful new series, THE BABY SHOWER, by Raye Morgan. Award-winning author Jennifer Greene also starts a new miniseries, THE STANFORD SISTERS, with the delightful *The Unwilling Bride.* For something a little different, take a peek at Joan Elliott Pickart's *Apache Dream Bride.* And the fun keeps on coming with Judith McWilliams's *Instant Husband,* the latest in THE WEDDING NIGHT series. Our Debut Author promotion introduces you to Amanda Kramer, author of the charmingly sexy *Baby Bonus.*

And you'll be excited to know that there's more **CELEBRATION 1000** next month, as the party continues with six more scintillating love stories, including *The Accidental Bodyguard,* a MAN OF THE MONTH from Ann Major.

Silhouette Desire—the passion continues! Enjoy!

Lucia Macro

Senior Editor

Please address questions and book requests to:
Silhouette Reader Service
U.S.: 3010 Walden Ave., P.O. Box 1325, Buffalo, NY 14269
Canadian: P.O. Box 609, Fort Erie, Ont. L2A 5X3

JENNIFER GREENE
THE UNWILLING BRIDE

SILHOUETTE *Desire*®
Published by Silhouette Books
America's Publisher of Contemporary Romance

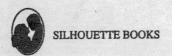

SILHOUETTE BOOKS

ISBN 0-373-75998-3

THE UNWILLING BRIDE

Books by Jennifer Greene

Silhouette Desire

Body and Soul #263
Foolish Pleasure #293
Madam's Room #326
Dear Reader #350
Minx #366
Lady Be Good #385
Love Potion #421
The Castle Keep #439
Lady of the Island #463
Night of the Hunter #481
Dancing in the Dark #498
Heat Wave #553
Slow Dance #600
Night Light #619
Falconer #671
Just Like Old Times #728
It Had To Be You #756
Quicksand #786
*Bewitched #847
*Bothered #855
*Bewildered #861
A Groom for Red Riding Hood #893
Single Dad #931
Arizona Heat #966
†*The Unwilling Bride* #998

Silhouette Intimate Moments

Secrets #221
Devil's Night #305
Broken Blossom #345
Pink Topaz #418

Silhouette Books

Birds, Bees and Babies 1990
"Riley's Baby"

*Jock's Boys
†The Stanford Sisters

JENNIFER GREENE

lives near Lake Michigan with her husband and two children. Before writing full-time, she worked as a teacher and a personnel manager. Michigan State University honored her as an "outstanding woman graduate" for her work with women on campus.

Ms. Greene has written more that forty category romances, for which she has won numerous awards, including the RITA for Best Short Contemporary Book, and both a Best Series Author and a Lifetime Achievement Award from *Romantic Times*.

Dear Reader,

I can still remember finding the first Silhouette Desire novel in the bookstores...and rushing home to put my feet up and savor those pages!

I moved to Silhouette over a decade ago. This is "home" for me, and I couldn't be more thrilled to be part of our **Celebration 1000.** When I write a Desire novel, I feel as if I'm talking to a fellow sister. I know you. You believe in love and commitment the way I do; you believe in families and healthy relationships...and you have the same problems I do as a woman living in the nineties. My books are *to* you as well as *about* you—and that caring between reader and writer is something that someone outside the romance field probably wouldn't understand. Romances are about us—our struggles, our hopes, our needs. I never had to "work" to create a heroine...she's every one of you, coping with the problems and trials of a woman today, striving to make the best life she can—and hopefully with a special lover, a man who deserves her.

I see our **Celebration 1000** as a celebration of you— all of you Desire readers are the heroines of today. We share our dreams together in every love story.

My best wishes to all of you.

Jennifer Greene

One

Someone was violently knocking on her front door, which Paige Stanford ignored. The phone had been ringing incessantly for the past hour, which she'd blithely ignored, too.

Growing up, her sisters used to tease her that she was so absentminded that she'd probably forget her own wedding. Paige had always vociferously resented that accusation. She wasn't in the *least* absentminded. She simply had a gift for intense concentration.

Like now.

Heaven knew what time it was. Paige wasn't sure when she had last eaten, either—and didn't care.

Watery winter sunlight poured through the south windows on the bench counter and cement floor. Her whole workshop was strewn with veiners, gravers, chisels and pumice stones, grindstones and Eskimo stylers, drills and sanders and files. None of it would make a lick of sense to anyone but her. A stranger had no way to understand that sometimes it took chaos and a dusty mess to create a treasure of incomparable beauty.

Her eyes were riveted on the exquisite piece of jade. Weeks ago, the jade had been nothing more than a jagged lump of stone.

Now it was a finished cameo.

Paige couldn't take her eyes off it. She'd made the cameo for her older sister, Gwen, whose birthday was six months away. Starting the project so far ahead was necessary, because it could so easily go wrong. There was no way of knowing, ever, what an innocuous lump of stone or shell would turn into until she started carving. Every stone held a mystery. Years ago she'd picked up an old saying in the sculpting world: "The truth is always there. You don't have to find it. All you have to do is carve away what isn't the truth."

Discovering that truth was what she loved—and what challenged her—but Paige knew better than to claim credit for the result. Maybe it took talent and skill to reveal the stone's secrets, but either there was beauty and truth intrinsic to the raw material or there wasn't. As it happened, this particular piece of jade had hidden a damn near breathtaking treasure.

But holy kamoly. When she'd stepped back to study the finished cameo, it was as if a ghost had walked on her shadow. Her arms still had goose bumps, and her pulse had picked up an uneasy, disturbing beat. Her whole work studio seemed flooded with an eerie silence. She felt edgy and unsettled, almost . . . frightened.

Normally it took an avalanche to shake Paige—and she'd have been real annoyed at the avalanche. She couldn't even remember being scared since she was sixteen, and that was an incident that had totally changed her life around. She was a practical, no-nonsense, unbudgeably tough cookie these days, and for Pete's sake, she'd made hundreds of cameos. To have some strange emotional reaction to this one was not only stupid but downright confounding.

Someone thunderously knocked on her front door again. The sound registered like the vaguely annoying buzz of a gnat. She heard it. She just paid no attention.

With an impatient scowl, she examined and reexamined the piece from every angle. There had to be a *reason* the cameo was giving her the willies. Paige being Paige, wasn't about to drop the problem until she figured it out.

The slab was a rough oval, perhaps ten inches across, and the image that had gradually emerged from the stone was simply a scene with a woman. Nothing frightening about her. Nothing weird. Like some primitive woods maiden, the woman was bent over a pond of water, gazing at her reflection with an expression as if she were discovering what she looked like for the first time. She was bare, sitting with her legs tucked under her, the carving revealing full breasts and the slender slope of her spine. A mane of long, flowing hair streamed down her back. Her profile revealed a sensual classic beauty—high cheekbones, a slim nose, mysterious deep-set eyes. Something in those eyes spoke of innocence, a woman untouched by man, yet that innocence was a striking contrast to the inherent sexuality and sensuality in everything else about her.

Paige reached up and scratched her chin. The piece was good. Beyond good. It was totally wrong for her sister—Gwen was unshakably traditional and would have a conniption fit at the nudity. Paige never set out to carve the woman with bare boobs; it was just how the stone came out. Thankfully she had enough time to make an entirely different gift for her sister, but that problem shouldn't take away from her own artistic sense of satisfaction. Without question, the cameo was one of the best things she'd ever done. She'd lucked out. The jade had magic. And it was always a thrill when she found a stone's secrets were this wondrous, this precious.

Except for this time. For some absolutely ridiculous reason, her hands were trembling.

From her denim overalls to the calfskin Uggs on her feet to the long, practical braid hanging over her shoulder, Paige wasn't the trembling type. All her life she'd been a rebel. As a teenager, she'd taken that too far, but as an adult she'd been grateful for those sturdy New England individualist genes. If she hadn't had the guts to beat to her own drummer, she'd never have had the courage to take up cameo carving as a profession. Being a little weird didn't bother her, but at the vast age of twenty-seven, she'd never been so ditzy as to believe in the fanciful or impossible.

The woman in the cameo appeared painfully familiar, when she couldn't be. Paige could not possibly know that woman, that face, that scene. The stone revealed its own secrets, and those secrets had nothing to do with the artist—no sculptor could impose or force an idea that wasn't inherent in the raw material.

The woman had no special meaning for her. Couldn't. Period. *Pfft.* End of subject.

So why couldn't she shake this stupid, silly, and damnably eerie déjà vu feeling?

For a few moments, she was vaguely aware that the repetitive pounding on her front door had finally ceased. But then a new sound intruded in the background. Apparently her unwanted visitor had entered the house, because she heard a voice calling out. A deep, booming, male voice—positively one she didn't recognize—coming from the muffled distance of the front hall.

On a scale of one to ten, her interest in chitchatting with a stranger was a negative five. Paige figured it was an even-Steven chance the guy would take off if he found no one home, and she was hidden pretty good. The workshop had once been a porch off a spare bedroom, tacked on to the old Vermont farmhouse as if it were a surprise and handily buried at the end of a wing. She didn't imagine a thief would choose to announce his presence with a big booming yell, so it was mighty unlikely the stranger represented any threat worth worrying about, and she was loath to break her concentration on the cameo if she had a choice.

It seemed she didn't.

Faster than gossip could spread bad news, the intruder barreled through her workshop doorway. Paige only had a few seconds to form an impression before all hell broke loose.

A slim memory slapped in her mind of someone— maybe Joanne, the clerk at the grocery store?—mentioning that she had a new neighbor who'd rented the old Jasper place down the road. In a tiny Vermont town like Walnut Woods, Paige knew every face and kissing cousin in the whole burg, so this had to be the newcomer.

Positively, though, Joanne had neglected to mention that the man was genetic kin to a bear. Wild, shaggy black hair framed a ruddy face with high Slavic cheekbones. A thick, wiry beard hid his chin. His eyes were piercing black with the shine of wet onyx. She really only had time for one quick glance—she guessed his age in the early thirties, definitely a man and not a boy—and one fast eyeful took in the cossack boots, the tree-trunk solid torso that stretched well past six feet, and the red-and-black flannel jacket that was dusted with snow and flapping open.

The devil spotted her and started yelling. Roaring, more like. She couldn't understand a word—she guessed the foreign language was Russian, because he seemed to be bellowing at her in all consonants—and offhand, she suspicioned he was communicating primarily in swear words. His voice volume was accompanied by wild pantomiming gestures indicating he wanted her to come with him. *Now.*

Paige never obeyed anyone—which he couldn't know—but the man had to have a rich fantasy life to assume any woman with a brain would obediently take off with a madman of a stranger. Still, he was a strikingly sexy hunk. His breathtaking looks had no relevance to anything. It was just a point of interest; she didn't run into a lot of men who could make a nun's hormones sizzle. If she *had* to be interrupted, he was uncontestably the most fascinating intrusion she'd had in a blue moon.

She waved a hand in a soothing gesture, hoping to calm him down. It was more than obvious that the stranger was overheated, uncontrolled, and beside himself about something. Whatever upset him clearly had to be addressed before she had a prayer of getting rid of him.

"Do you speak English?" she asked.

That stopped him short. "Da . . . yes." As if he just then recognized that he was speaking to her in the wrong language, he threw up his hands. The gesture was as exuberantly extravagant as everything else about him. Lowering his voice two volumes, he said clearly and succinctly, "My beautiful lambchop, your kitchen is on fire."

She blinked.

No one—but no one—had ever called Paige "lambchop." She'd never even heard such a sexist term in a decade. Whoever had taught the stranger English must either have been ancient or had a mischievous sense of humor—who knew if he realized what he was saying?—but then the meaning of his words registered.

She sniffed. Fast. Sometimes, when she worked with power tools, her workshop picked up a leftover, dusty smoke smell. But this scrabbling hint of smoke wasn't at all the same odor. And it definitely wasn't emanating from her workroom.

"Aw, shoot," she muttered, and took off. Guilt pumped extra adrenaline through her veins. She hit the turn in the hall at a near gallop. No question she'd put a loaf of bread in the oven to bake earlier. She didn't make her own bread often, but something about all the kneading and pounding and mess invariably inspired the creative juices when she was in a work slump. And it worked that morning, too. She clearly remembered flying back to her shop and diving back into her cameo project with renewed and furiously intense concentration.

She'd just sort of accidentally forgotten about the bread.

The bear tagged her heels as she tore down the white-stucco hall and rounded the corner toward the kitchen. Smoke belched through the room, thicker than cumulus clouds, and at a glance she could see flames shooting from the old wood stove.

A woman who lost track of time as often as she did learned to be an ace pro with emergencies. Her judgment call was quick and came from experience—this wasn't a 911 problem requiring outside help. It was just a run-of-the-mill ordinary disaster. Coughing—and calling herself a number of colorful names—she raced toward the old-fashioned broom closet and yanked out the giant fire extinguisher.

For an instant there, she'd forgotten she had a side kick. The stranger suddenly leaped into action, as if his first concern had been rescuing any humans in the house, and his second was an automatic assumption that he was needed to take charge. The bear grabbed the extinguisher from her hands and then pushed her—right in the chest!—out of harm's way through the door.

He shouted something at her, but it was in consonants again. He tried a second time. "I need...cloth! You got cloth thingie?"

She interpreted that he wanted hot pads before opening the oven, but he found the pads on his own. They were in plain sight on the counter, just like about everything else in the old fashioned blue-and-white kitchen. Paige firmly *believed* in a clean, neat, everything-put-away cooking space. She just never got around to *doing* it. Good thing, this time, because he found the hot pads and hurled the flaming bread pan in the snow in a matter of seconds. Then he pulled the pin on the extinguisher and let it rip inside the oven.

The fire was out and the hoopla over almost faster than she could spit. The kitchen was still choking from the stench of the burned bread and acrid extinguisher spray, but even that was dissipating quickly. Her stranger hadn't slowed down yet. One window was already cracked open—her wood stove could toast a small country if there was an outlet for the heat—but now he threw up the sashes on all the rest of the windows. Nice, freezing, seventeen-degree Vermont winter air poured into the room like a blessing.

Her heart was still slamming, so it took a few seconds to get her breath back and assess the damages. The ancient wood stove had a fresh, new coat of blacking, but the old baby had survived fires before. A few more soot stains only added to its character. For the hundredth time she consoled herself that her gift for intense concentration was a wonderful thing, not a dismally disgusting character flaw. Her life would just run smoother if she paid an eensy bit more attention to real life. Thank God, though, it really didn't appear that there was any serious harm done.

The bear seemed to reach the same conclusion. He whipped around and pinned her with a studying stare. "You okay, fruitcake?"

She blinked. Again.

"Ah. Fruitcake is wrong word, I know." He thought fast. "Cupcake. You okay, my cupcake?"

She dry-washed her face with a hand. It didn't seem the time to suggest some changes in his vocabulary to adjust for twentieth century feminist American values. Not before they'd even been introduced. And not while he was beaming at her with a big, brawny, unnervingly sexy grin that somehow made her...rattled.

"I saw smoke from my house. Just little bit, coming from you one open window. Good thing I saw that, huh, lambchop? All gone now. No hurt done. You okay, you house okay, happy to be of rescue." He held out his hand. "I am Stefan Michaelovich. Your neighbor."

"Paige Stanford. And I'm grateful that you spotted the smoke so quickly. Thank you for, um, rescuing me." Returning his handshake was just basic manners. Paige had no idea how such an innocuous, automatic courtesy turned into something else.

His palm clapped against hers and then just laid there—he didn't pump or shake; he just held her hand in a capturing squeeze. Perhaps people shook hands differently in Russia? She had no problem with that. It was just that the connection was tighter than a plug in a socket, and she wasn't prepared for the electric shock.

His hand was swallowing bigger than hers, and warm. His grip had all the muscular power of a physically active man, yet his skin was smooth and unscarred, his nails pared short and clean. By contrast, her hands were a disgrace. Nothing new. Unavoidably she picked up calluses and cuts from working so many hours with chisels and carving tools. She never thought about her hands—who cared?—but she was suddenly, strangely conscious of every knuckle and nail, every surface of texture that touched his.

Seconds spun out. She kept expecting him to release her hand. Instead his eyes charged over her face as the warmth of his palm seeped into hers. A clock

ticked somewhere. Radiators clanked on. Cold, sharp
air gushed from the windows, rapidly obliterating the
last of the smoke, and still his gaze honed on her face,
stalking every feature as if fascinated by her eyes and
nose and mouth.

She had an ordinary nose. Plain old brown eyes. An
average mouth with no lipstick or gloss. Her bulky
denim overalls entirely concealed her figure, and by
this time in the day the single braid dangling down her
back was undoubtedly sloppy and askew.

Years and years ago, Paige couldn't find a skirt tight
enough, a sweater skimpy enough, but that was back
when she'd been a wild, reckless girl who was determined to test and tease her new feminine powers on
every passing boy. She'd wiped every trace of that
teenage girl off the map. Fiercely. Completely. Eons
ago. There was nothing suggestive about her appearance now—absolutely nothing.

Yet the stranger seemed to find something in her
looks that captivated him. He wouldn't stop looking
at her, his attention absorbed, as if he were learning
things about her from the nest of their palms and the
look of her face. Things she didn't know. Things she
didn't see when she looked in a mirror.

"Mr. Michaelovich—" she began uneasily.

He swiftly corrected her. "Stefan."

"Stefan, then. I—" But abruptly she forgot whatever she'd planned to say, because that simply, he re-
leased her hand and she was free again. Those few
seconds of unnerving silence might never have been.
The way he looked at her, the brush of those midnight black eyes on her face and body, the electric plug
of awareness between his palm and hers...she must
have, simply must have, imagined it.

She drew herself up to her full five foot seven inches, and mentally scrambled for something intelligent and neighborly to say. There wasn't a man in Walnut Woods that she didn't get along with; she never had a problem relating with a guy one-on-one—and he certainly wasn't going to be the exception. "So...you're living in the old Jasper place?"

"Yes. Just down your road."

Since that seemed to awkwardly end the conversation, she scrambled for something more. "Are you here with your wife and family?"

A slow waltz of a smile. He was pleased she'd asked. "No wife. No small ones. But the Borges in town—they are family, third cousins, maybe four. They are how I came here, to your Vermont, instead of L.A. or Georgia or Texas. This was only place I had a family from Russia, so good to start from."

"You plan to stay?"

"To stay in America—oh, yes. I am already studying to become citizen. But am only living in Walnut Woods for couple months, temporary until I figure out jobs and where best to settle. My work is physics. For now I have computer hooked up, real cool, real groovy, can do much work this way. In the long time, though, I will need to find my own kind."

Although his accent was thick, he wasn't that hard to understand. She mentally translated "in the long time" to mean "in the long run" and almost chuckled at his use of the ancient "groovy" slang. It was just his last comment that she couldn't comprehend. "By your own kind, do you mean other Russian people?"

"No, no. Being Russian, not important. French, German, Japanese, would make no difference, either.

I mean finding other people in physics, like me, a lab or university where we talk the same work. This is why I come here. Important, this freedom and right to talk with each other. We have many, many problems affecting whole planet. Cannot fix these nature of problems unless we all have freedom to talk together. So I come to America to melt in your pot." He hesitated. "Have I said it right, about melt in the pot?"

"Right enough. The phrase is 'melting pot'. People say that America is a melting pot of different cultures." He sounded like a hard-core idealist, she mused, which somehow didn't surprise her any more than his physicist background. Never mind the overwhelming shoulders and that wild beard. He only appeared to be an uncivilized bear at first glance. He hadn't missed anything yet. Those black eyes were shrewd, swift, sharp with intelligence—and maybe saw too much for a woman's own good.

"I struggle. Reading the language, no problem, and the words in my work, I know. But talking everyday words . . ." He shook his head with an exuberant grin. "Your language can make me tired quick."

"You're doing fine," she assured him.

"Nyet. Will take time. But I get there. Will be happy when I get past all this struggling part." He shifted on his feet and looked around again. "Well . . . you want help cleaning up this mess?"

"No, no. I can handle it myself."

"Could have had big fire. You work hard concentrating, you forget things like fire, huh? No one else here? Like husband?"

"No, I live alone." Everyone in town knew she lived by herself, so there was no point in being less than honest.

"Hmm." She wasn't sure what he was assessing with that long, lingering hmm, but his gaze was suddenly all over her face again. Then, with one swift move, he pushed away from the counter and loped for the door. "Well, I go home. But you know now I live close if you need help, yes?"

"Yes. And that's very kind." She followed him to the door and had just grabbed for the knob when he suddenly pivoted around.

"If it's an okeydoke, I would sure like to get it on with you, babe."

Her jaw had to drop a full inch.

"Uh-oh. I say something to offend? I mean to say... hope to see you again. Hope you might put up with my learning new English sometimes? Be like neighbors, friends?"

"I... sure."

A flash of another high-voltage grin, and then—finally—he was gone. Paige closed the door behind him with a massive sigh of relief. She shook her head. Of course he hadn't meant that "get it on with you, babe" in a sexual context.

Stefan was obviously having some problems coping with a new language. That someone had taught him a ton of colloquial expressions wasn't helping. He undoubtedly didn't realize what he was saying.

The room was freezing—no surprise, with all the open windows—and Paige abruptly hustled to shag them all down and latch them again. When she reached the far south pane, though, she yanked down the window and then hesitated. From that view she could still see him, his shaggy head thrown back as he chugged down her snowy driveway, past the old stone fence until he crossed the road out of sight.

Vermont was Robert Frost country, and her stone fence was typical of a New England neighborhood that strongly believed Frost's philosophy about good fences making good neighbors. Her friends and neighbors all knew she was a hopeless hermit—a happy hermit—and respected her workaholic habits. Everyone knew better than to interrupt her workday.

Somehow she didn't think the gregarious Russian had ever read Frost.

As she ambled back toward her workshop, she told herself it didn't matter. They weren't likely to run into each other that often. Positively, though, it would be cruel to be unfriendly when they did. If he blithely ran around calling women "babe" and "cupcake" and boisterously suggesting "they get it on," some woman was going to lynch him.

It wouldn't kill her to give him a little language coaching. He had to be lonely, trying to adjust to a new country, a new place, new ways.

Paige knew about loneliness. She knew all about having trouble fitting in. Old memories suddenly pushed through her mind like bubbles rising to the surface of a pond. She pushed them back down.

At twenty-seven, she was secure and content with her life-style. Maybe she'd once been as flighty as a fickle wind, but that unfortunate period in her life was long over. These days, nothing budged her from her steady course—except, of course, for that dadblasted strange cameo waiting for her attention in the workshop. Her mind turned to her sisters and to the work waiting for her.

Her new neighbor was about as restful as a tornado. But he was basically just a stranger passing through. No one she needed to worry about. No one who was going to affect her life.

Paige had survived tornadoes before.

Two

The computer screen glowed in the dark, illuminating a complex jumble of mathematical numbers and equations. *"No, no, no"* Stefan typed on the keyboard. *"Four years ago, discovered this didn't work. Look at line 47. The problem in logic begins there...."*

When he finished with the post, he leaned back and rubbed his tired eyes. The mathematician he'd been communicating with lived in Paris, outside the Sorbonne. Through the wonders of a computer, modem and an internet connection, Stefan could teach or argue theory or share ideas with some of the finest scientific minds in the world.

He'd been in America three weeks. Long enough to discover that freedom was far more addictive than any drug. He couldn't get enough of it.

Growing up in Russia, he had been isolated because of his brain. Patriotism had been drilled into him when he was young—his mind belonged to the state. Forget a movie with popcorn; forget falling in love; forget taking a passel of kids sledding on a snowy afternoon. His brain was a gift, and he had a responsibility to produce for his country, to channel all his drive and abilities toward that goal.

Stefan had no quarrel with any of that. He'd accepted the loneliness, accepted his responsibilities. He never saw the conflict coming that would slowly eat him alive. But physics was his field. Energy. In a world with finite resources, energy problems—and solutions—had increasing power over war, peace, economics, quality of life. Solutions existed, if scientific minds across the world could simply talk together, share what they knew. Repression of knowledge was alien to everything he believed in. Suffering had no country. Certain problems were universal and had no flag. And when he'd had a breakthrough, and discovered he would not be permitted to share his research with other physicists across the world, that was the straw that had broken the donkey's back.

He'd started saving his rubles. Enough to give him a solid nest egg in America. It took a long time—too long—but the waiting had intensified his feelings and his resolve. America was his country long before he set foot on her soil.

Impatiently he flicked off the computer. The living room flooded with darkness. For a few minutes, there was no sound in the whole house beyond the rumbling of the furnace and the rhythmic tick of a distant clock. As his eyes slowly dilated, he focused on the view from his window, where the snowy landscape was mystically glazed by moonlight. Down the winding road, he saw lights. *Her* lights.

Thinking about Paige had started to drive him crazy.

He lurched out of his desk chair and ambled to the casement windows. Paige slept in the corner room on the second story of the old brick farmhouse. He guessed the location of her bedroom, because lights never emanated from any other room on that floor at night.

Right now, it was just nine o'clock, and the second story was predictably blacker than pitch. She hadn't gone to bed yet. But she would—around a quarter to eleven. Her bedtime rituals were as regular as a heartbeat.

Stefan never meant to make a pattern of watching her. One night he'd just happened to glance out, and caught her standing in the window with the light behind her, as she took down her braid. Her house was four hundred yards distance from his, not close enough to see clearly, but close enough to appease his conscience about being a voyeur. He had never seen anything he shouldn't. She was never naked. Never remotely unclothed. In fact, she seemed to favor sleeping in some big, voluminous garment that resembled a feed sack.

Personally he thought she belonged in satin.

Taking down her hair was the last chore she did before sleeping. She stood at the window, stargazing while her fingers unplaited the long, tangled braid. Then she brushed her hair, always with swift, impatient movements, as if doing a necessary job for the sole purpose of getting it over with.

Personally, he would have brushed her hair quite differently.

When her hair was finally loose, it streamed down her back in a waterfall, past her shoulder blades, as rich as mink, silken, glossy. A man could go crazy, imagining his hands in that hair. Her arms were raised when she brushed back from the crown, and even in that appalling sackcloth garment, her breasts pushed and thrust against the fabric. A man could go crazy, imagining his hands on those firm, full breasts.

She couldn't be a virgin. Stefan had carefully studied all the American newspapers. He wasn't sure how old Paige was, maybe mid-twenties. But it was clear no American women were virgins past the age of sixteen. They talked about sex everywhere: ads, TV, movies, national news. Stefan figured he could not assimilate into the culture until he figured such things out—he would not want to offend some woman sometime by accidentally inferring that she did not have reams of sexual prowess and expertise. This was hard. In his country, it was okay if a woman had not slept with the entire Bronco Bills baseball team. Here, a guy might be considered disgustingly repressed if he failed to talk about sex—or worse, if he considered sex to be an intimately private subject. Stefan was trying hard to get on the band tire.

Paige, though, struck him as being on a different band tire, too. Though it seemed impossible, he couldn't shake the impression that she was asleep as a woman.

He'd seen her working attire—no makeup, the tight braid, the bulky, concealing clothes. Yet it was only natural that she would choose practical, common sense clothing styles with her work. There was a storm of dreams in her dark brown eyes, the passion of emotion. Her movements had an inherent sensuality and grace. And her face had a classic beauty, a damn near mesmerizing beauty, yet she seemed completely unaware of her looks, or how those looks could affect a man.

The morning of the fire, he'd seen the jade cameo in her workshop. It was her. Exactly her. At the time, he hadn't realized it because his mind had been on the fire. But later, the profile in that jade cameo had come back to haunt him. Later, he'd considered that a woman who created cameos had to have a deeply romantic nature.

Yet she lived alone. Stefan kept an eye out, not just from nosiness but because if she was so absent-minded as to start one fire, she could certainly start another. No one watched out for her. No men came calling. She worked all the time, and only seemed to leave the house for groceries. Yet night after night, watching her in that window, he'd seen her vulnerability and loneliness.

He knew loneliness well, but there had always been reasons why it had been difficult to pursue a mate in his life. It was a mind-boggling puzzle why she didn't have a man in hers.

For three weeks, that puzzle had been gnawing on his mind.

Longer than a man who thrived on challenges could be reasonably expected to stand.

Swiftly he turned his head from the window. His gaze pounced on the telephone. He'd mastered the telephone book his first week in America, read the entire Yellow Pages one night. Finding the number for "Stanford, Paige" was a piece of cake. He considered for a minute, then dialed her number and carried the telephone over to the window.

She answered the phone on the fourth ring, but her voice sounded husky and breathless as if she'd been running. "Paige here."

"This is Stefan. I not bother you long. I guess you are working—"

"Yes, I was, actually—"

"Just one quick question. When you call police here, you don't call police, right? You call 9-1-1? That's how?"

"Yes, for an emergency, that's exactly h—"

"Okeydoke. Not bother you further. Thank you for the neighborly help, my cupcake." Gently he hung up the receiver and waited. He counted to ten in English, then French, then started in Russian with *aden, dva, tree, chaterrie*... the telephone jangled next to him.

As innocent as a virgin, he picked it up. "Stefan here," he barked, adopting her method of answering.

Her words gushed out like water tumbling from a faucet. "Stefan, for heaven's sake, are you in some kind of trouble? Do you need help?"

He stroked his beard, thinking he should probably be feeling big guilt for trying such a ruse. Perhaps the guilt would come. Momentarily he was captured by the sound of her voice. "You would help if I were in trouble? You barely know me?"

"We're neighbors. In America, neighbors help each other."

"This is wonderful quality," he said. "We need to spread this American quality of kindness across the world. It would make a difference."

He heard her release a quick sigh. A lustily, loud impatient sigh. Full of passion. "Stefan, we can talk about philosophy another time. I was worried why you wanted to dial 911. Did you have a break-in?"

"Break-in? I don't know this phrase."

"Did you have a robbery? A thief?"

"No, no. No break-in. I am just figuring out how to do things. Not easy. I had much trouble in the grocery store today. Nothing is the same here. I like everything, you understand, this is my country now. But being able to read fluently and talk fluently is not the same, and I seem to be culturally gapped big-time."

He heard her make another sound—the chortling hint of a chuckle.

"You would laugh at my problem?" he asked her.

"Oh, no." She sobered quickly. "No, Stefan, I wasn't laughing at you—"

"I worry fiercely about offending by saying wrong things, doing wrong things. But this is truth—I am utter confusion." He didn't have to work to make his tone sound mournful. A little talent for drama was in his Russian genes. "How kind, your neighborly offer to help. Much welcomed."

"Ummmm..."

"I am close to desperate in this confusion, so your offer to help could not arrive at better time. I feel relief. Big relief. Be over in five minutes to accept this help, maybe quicker."

Actually it didn't take him four minutes to burrow into a jacket, hike the snowy road, leap her fence and exuberantly knock on her door. When she opened it, her face had an expression of bewilderment as if she had no idea how this impromptu visit came to be.

Stefan stomped the snow off his boots and closed the door—biting winter wind was gusting in the foyer. Then he smiled at her. Her forehead had a dusty smudge. Her thick brown braid had wisps escaping in a halo around her cheeks. Her black sweater had a hole, as did her jeans, and she was wearing socks, no shoes. But beneath all that was a breathtakingly beautiful woman, and it was a luxury to just look into those velvet brown eyes. "You still working so late, and here, I come and interrupt you. How about I make you something to drink while you keep working, so you not mind this interruption so bad?"

"It's okay," she said.

"You're not thirsty? Not hungry?"

Paige had no chance to consider whether she was hungry or thirsty. She wasn't sure if she was coming or going, by the time Stefan had been there an hour.

She vaguely recalled his exuberantly insisting that she continue working as if he weren't there. What a joke. Stefan was an impossible man to ignore. He'd raided her kitchen for a simple glass of water and emerged with a pot of hot coffee, a bottle of vodka under his arm, two mugs and a six-inch-high sandwich—for her. "You forgot to eat, yes?"

It was true—she had forgotten dinner—and because there was no convenient place to set up the snack in her work studio, they'd ended up in the living room.

There'd been no lights on. He'd switched on her grandmother's ruby thumbnail globe lamp. There'd been no fire in the fieldstone hearth, but he'd fixed that, too—stacked the wood, checked the flue and then lit a match to the kindling. He'd tossed her some couch pillows, pushed a claw-foot stool under her feet and had tipped the vodka bottle into her coffee mug a couple of times now.

"Cold tonight," he kept saying. "As cold as Petersburg in a blizzard. Need to warm your toes."

Her toes *were* cold, not from temperature but from nerves. Stefan seemed to have settled in as solidly as an oak tree taking root. It wasn't exactly as if he were pushy. It was more like being stuck with a big, effusively friendly bear. Somewhere in that gnarly, wild beard was a boyish grin, a winsomeness—he was clearly trying to help her, to please. It was just...those weren't a boy's eyes looking her over by the lap of firelight.

Paige kept telling herself to bury the silly nerves. She'd been working all day, looked like something the cat would refuse to bring home. There was no reason to think he was attracted, no reason not to share a companionable drink with a neighbor. Stefan had thrown himself in the overstuffed blue recliner, a nice three feet away. He hadn't said one word on any other subject but the reason he came—and heaven knew, he *did* need help with the language.

"...so I pay this woman, and I say 'thank you, we hit the sack anytime, chick.'" Stefan shrugged. "Something clearly wrong with what I say. I meant compliment. But she turned color of roses, real quick, real red, and started talking so fast I couldn't follow. I don't know what went wrong."

"Oh, Stefan." Paige shook her head. "Who taught you English?"

"I learned in school, from early days. But that was always reading more than speaking. In university years, I met Ivan. A friend, a physicist, thirty years older than me, but he had actually lived in America. He knew the real English, the kind people spoke every day. Nothing like textbooks. I studied with him, hard."

"Um... Stefan," she said tactfully, "he taught you a lot of slang."

"Yes, slang, thank God. I discovered on instant arrival that no one here speaks with grammar. Learning all that grammar useless. I am relieved to know slang. I not want to stick out like sore toe."

"Sore thumb." Paige corrected him automatically, and then hesitated, unsure how to approach his language misconceptions without hurting his feelings. "About your friend... I'm sure he was a really wonderful friend, and I certainly don't mean to criticize him... but I'm afraid he taught you some slang expressions that aren't used anymore. Especially some of the phrases referring to women."

"Yeah?" Stefan was clearly one of those high-energy, physical men who couldn't sit still for more than two seconds. Not for the first time, he sprang from the recliner, checked her mug, noted it was empty and splashed in another double dose of vodka and coffee. More coffee than vodka this time, she hoped. "Explain to me some examples, okay?"

"Well, the thing is, Stefan, if your friend lived here a long time ago, he just wouldn't have any reason to know that we've had a strong political women's movement in this country over the last couple of decades. There was a time it was okay to call a woman cupcake or chick or doll. In another time, those were terms of endearment or affection—"

Stefan's shaggy eyebrows shot up in surprise. "Endearments are now forbidden? American women no longer want affection?"

"No, no. It's not that. It's just that certain terms have become symbols of women being oppressed."

"Paige, you are throwing me for a rope. I know about oppression. Oppression has nothing in common with word meaning of affection, not that I understand. You American women seek to oppress affection?"

"No. No, I..." She shook her head, starting to feel utterly confused herself. "The point is that some of those words and phrases became symbols. Symbols of the ways women had been treated like sex objects."

"Ah. I get you. Much clearer now." He hesitated. "I think. What is sex object?"

Paige grabbed her mug. She'd been wrong. No matter what proportion of vodka he'd splashed into the coffee, it wasn't enough. Not nearly enough to be comfortable with the unexpected turn this conversation was taking. She slugged down a gulp of the brew and grappled to explain. "A sex object is when someone is treated like a thing instead of a person. Women wanted to be valued for more than just their bodies or looks. They wanted to be valued and loved for their minds."

"Yeah? So what is the news here? This is automatic. What man with brain would love half the woman? Why waste time loving less than body, soul, mind, whole caboodle? How else would you love?"

"Um, maybe we'd better try this language lesson another time," Paige said desperately. Her conscience shot her slivers of guilt for copping out. Before he went to town again—for his sake—he really needed to understand that it wasn't wise to call strange women "cupcake" or warmly suggest that they "get it on" or "hit the sack." But to summarize the whole history of feminist philosophy and politically correct language in a short conversation—it just wasn't that easy. There was clearly a whole difference in cultures.

Or there was a difference in him. An image flashed through her mind of Stefan, making love, inhaling a woman's mind, body, soul, "whole caboodle." Blood charged through her veins in an embarrassing rush. He had sounded so matter-of-fact. Maybe loving "whole caboodle" was status quo for him, but it wasn't anything she was familiar with. And she was utterly confounded how the subject had veered in such an intimately personal direction. They'd started out in the nice, cool North Pole—how had they ended up in the hot climate of Tahiti?

"You are probably frustrated with me. I learn too slow," he said morosely.

"No, no, you learn very fast. It's just that learning certain things about any language probably takes a lot of time."

"Yes, exactly true. But it helps much having someone to explain. I hope we can talk like this again?"

"Sure," Paige said. What else could she say? She had a bad feeling she'd only further confused him about the language instead of helping him this time. Still, she carefully added, "I'm afraid I don't have a lot of free time, though, Stefan. I work long hours."

"I understand. I saw your workroom, your cameos. Maybe you could show me something about your art another time, too, okeydoke?"

"Okeydoke." When he surged to his feet, Paige abruptly realized that he was leaving—without having to be asked, which was a huge relief—and she swiftly uncurled from the couch and popped to her feet, too. She opened her mouth, intending to say something cordial about his stopping by. Instead a giggle bubbled from her throat and escaped. A giggle. Her. A plain old girlish, giddy, happy giggle. How appallingly silly.

Stefan threw back his head and laughed. "You sleep good tonight, babe. Vodka good for you. Nothing to worry, *lyubemaya*. Great medicine for the soul."

Paige didn't know what that *lyubemaya* meant, but knowing his fondness for affectionate terms, she figured it was too dangerous to ask. Temporarily her reaction to a couple of spiked coffees was embarrassing her to death. At five foot seven and a sturdy one hundred and thirty pounds, she certainly should have been able to handle a little alcohol. For that matter, she'd never been a sissy drinker, had always taken her brandy in straight shots anytime she had a cold. It just belatedly occurred to her that she hadn't had a cold in three or four years. "I'm afraid I haven't had much experience with vodka," she admitted.

"And I bet you never had borscht? Caviar? Solyanka? We will have to fix all those missing experiences in your life very soon."

Food, he was talking about. Not love. Not sex. It had to be the hundred-proof liquid sloshing in her mind that made her suddenly think of "missed experiences" in a context with Stefan.

Vodka might be medicine for the soul in Russia, but it wasn't for her. Positively she was never touching the stuff again if it made her feel this... goofy.

Stefan had been nothing but friendly. A lonely man in a strange country, seeking some basic companionship. Even now, as he yanked on his alpaca jacket, the front hall sconce light illuminated his genial smile, the crinkle of laugh lines around his eyes. It was just his powerful stature that made her five-seven seem de-

fenselessly small. Maybe he was hopelessly gregarious, but he hadn't done or said one thing to make her
worry that he was anything but a kind man. A safe
man. A good guy.

"Snowing again," he noted, as he pulled worn
leather gloves from his pockets.

"We'll probably have a couple more inches by
morning." She hugged her arms under her chest. The
front hall was drafty cold. He was obviously ready to
leave, so she thought he was just turning toward her to
say goodbye. And she saw him bend his head, but she
also saw his kind, safe almost-familiar-now smile.

It never occurred to her that a kiss was coming.

It never occurred to her that he wanted to kiss her.

Her mind scrabbled to recall if she'd sent him any
come-on body language signals. But of course she
hadn't. Paige hadn't sent any men those willing body
language signals since she was sixteen. And lightning
storms weren't supposed to happen in the blizzard
month of January.

She wasn't prepared, never even got her arms un-
folded before they were trapped between his body and
hers. A big hand cupped her head. His lips touched
hers, more gentle than a whisper, his mouth unbearably soft against the tickle of his rough, wiry beard.

The taste of him was foreign. Alien. Drugging sweet
and disturbing. Her pulse zoomed like a skater on the
ice for the first time, unpredictable and unsteady and
flying way too fast.

That first skimming kiss turned deeper. His mouth
rubbed against hers, testing, exploring the texture of
her lips, savoring the taste of her. You'd think he
hadn't kissed a woman in the last hundred years.
You'd think he just discovered a secret treasure, and

her senses wrapped around the smell of leather and alpaca wool and the male warmth radiating from his body.

The speed of light was fast, but not half as fast as the speed of darkness. It had been so long since she'd kissed anyone. She'd forgotten. The exhilaration sweeping through her pulse was more frightening than any danger. She'd forgotten what it was like to feel that innocent burst of yearning, to feel that lusty dizzy spring-fever high, to feel that heady excitement of wanting. Or maybe she'd never known. She'd kissed boys, not men. Never a man who knew how to kiss like he did. Never *him*.

She meant to bolt, not close her eyes. She meant to push him away, not stand stock-still as if she were caught up in a spell of enchantment. She wasn't wild anymore. She'd slayed and buried every hint of wildness in her heart, years and years ago, yet it was as if she'd frozen those emotions instead of truly killing them off, because they seeped through her now, billowing loose like a parachute in the wind.

It was his fault. If she could just get a lungful of oxygen, she knew she could catch control again. Yet his thumb grazed the line of her jaw, in a caressing gesture as potent as tenderness. And his kiss turned openmouthed, claiming her response as if it already belonged to him, making her lips ache and her head feel thrumming dizzy.

She couldn't breathe, couldn't think. And then, she didn't have to. He lifted his head. There was a fire in his eyes that hadn't been there before, sharp and black and hot, yet he pushed back a strand of her hair with a gentle touch. His gaze scored her face, studying her eyes, her mouth, the flush burned in her cheeks that he'd put there. And then he smiled.

"Paige..." He dropped his hand and stepped toward the door, as if nothing but leaving had ever been on his mind. The sudden glint of humor in his eyes, in fact, had the devil's own mischief. "So you know. That was not about oppression or sex object. That was just Russian way of saying thank you, good night."

That was it. When he opened the door, a harsh sting of snow blasted in, but then he was gone.

She threw the latch and hooked the chain bolt, unsure whether she wanted to shoot him—or laugh. It would seem she'd gotten *one* language lesson through to him, if he understood the concepts of "oppression" and "sex object" well enough to joke about them.

She couldn't seem to laugh, though. Her heart was still slamming too hard. Even when he'd completely disappeared out of sight down the driveway, her pulse was still bouncing off the walls.

That Russian didn't need language to communicate a damn thing.

Abruptly she realized how late it was. She gathered up the dishes from the living room, then started turning off lights through the house. The last room was her workshop, and when she switched off the overhead from the doorway, her eyes instinctively flew to the jade cameo.

The light couldn't help but draw her. She'd stashed the jade cameo on a shelf, still unsure what she was going to do with it. But even with the whole downstairs dark, the bright snowy night caught the soft iridescent glow of the stone. It was the nature of jade to appear lit from within, and she found herself staring at the carved woman in profile, frowning hard, not really seeing her but simply thinking.

She used to be wild and impulsive, once upon a time. She used to be reckless, giddy on life and her newly developing powers as a woman, teasing every boy she could attract. And it was never far from her conscience, that a sixteen-year-old boy had once paid the cost for her thoughtlessness and insensitivity.

She'd changed. Completely. Her life was self-discipline, work, responsibility. Possibly she was a teensy bit absentminded—hey, there was no way to wipe every single flaw from her character—but she felt good about the woman she'd turned into. She hadn't hurt anyone. She'd been very careful of that. Her sisters said she was too tough on herself, but Paige stood on her own two feet, strong and sturdy.

Alone.

Safe.

Alone and safe had been paired in her mind for a decade, as natural as pairing peanut butter and jelly. Nothing she'd questioned . . . until tonight and a wild, wayward kiss that had come out of nowhere.

Around that unpredictable Russian, Paige thought darkly, she had better watch her p's and q's.

That settled, she pivoted on her heel and went up to bed.

Three

Paige was too busy working to think about Stefan.

Her legs were wrapped around the spokes of the work stool, her hands around a cup of fragrant Darjeeling tea. At five in the morning—when she had just as determinedly *not* been thinking about Stefan—she'd remembered the coral.

The chances of her falling back to sleep wouldn't make bookie's odds, and the coral was an excellent excuse to bolt out of bed. So she'd charged downstairs in old black sweats and bare feet, and burrowed through all the boxes of raw materials until she found it.

Sipping her tea—from the second pot, now—she studied the crooked, jagged wedge of coral shell with ruthless concentration. She still recalled the sly, sneaky grin on the clerk who sold her the piece—he'd been real sure he was pawning off a worthless piece on a rookie. Maybe the clerk was an ace pro at textbook geology, but he didn't know cameos and he didn't know coral.

She did.

In the middle of the night, when she'd been fighting to get that blasted Russian off her mind, she remembered the coral, remembered the break in the outer layer of the shell, the rich cherry red color the Italians called *rosso scuro*.

Coral was almost always uniform in color. Finding a piece with two shades was crying rare—and a cameo carver's dream. Further, the coral that mattered was gem material—true precious coral—not the stuff that came off from reefs in shallow seas, but the stuff that came from down deep. This piece came from down deep, off the coast of Sardinia. No holes, no flaws, no cracks. The shadings were rich and true. It'd make a pendant, nothing bigger, but the potential for treasure was there—and hopefully a perfect treasure for her sister, Gwen.

Paige gulped another sip of tea. Energy was biting at her harder than hunger. Her fingers itched to pick up a chisel and start working. But she had to know the piece of coral more intimately than her own heartbeat before touching it. Nothing was more fragile than coral. Nothing as easily broken.

Like her sister, she thought.

Her gaze strayed to the jade cameo on the top shelf. She'd really been stupid. It had always been a mistake, trying to make a present for Gwen in jade. Coral was so much more like her. Probably from its first discovery, coral had been symbolic in medicine and magic. A romantic talisman of beauty and the kind of beauty one put in everyday life, which was exactly like

Gwen. Hopelessly romantic. Fragile. Easily hurt, easily scarred, but beautiful on the inside—if anyone could ever get her to believe it.

Too restless to sit, Paige popped off the stool and started twisting the gooseneck stem of her work lamp so the light better illuminated every angle of the coral, her mind on Gwen—and Abby.

Paige had been badly worried about both sisters since Christmas. Generations of Stanfords had lived in the old Vermont homestead until the clan scattered—Abby and Gwen had grown up, moved away, and then their parents had retired to Arizona. The whole crew had argued with Paige about living alone in the old-fashioned, heat-eating monster, but this was home, the roots of the whole family, and they all still gathered here for the holidays. They had this past Christmas, too, but with mom and dad there, both her older sisters had kept a protective lid on any serious conversations.

Paige didn't need the specifics to recognize that both Gwen and Abby were stressed out and unhappy. Growing up, they'd all fought like snakes and mongeese. Still did. Gwen had made one man her whole life; Abby was all ambition and drive; and Paige was the unconventional rebel. Bickering and teasing was probably inevitable when none of them ever had one single thing in common, much less came close to sharing each others' goals or dreams.

It didn't matter. It never mattered. They didn't have to understand each other to love. The bond between sisters had always been unshakable. Paige always knew when one of them was unhappy. The reverse was just as true. And she'd been frustrated and worried ever since Christmas, that her sisters were having some kind of trouble in their personal lives that she couldn't do a damn thing about.

A cameo wasn't going to solve Gwen's problems. The need was in Paige, to create something for her sister, something that had meaning, something that expressed love. Impatiently she propped her hands on her hips, fiercely concentrating. All raw materials looked like nothing in the beginning. The coral, no different than other shells or stones she worked with, had a secret to tell. It was up to her to find the truth.

The frown on her forehead suddenly eased. Blood started waltzing through her veins. She had it. Automatically her fingers fumbled blind, yanking open the drawer on the left, groping for the India ink pen and the leather-lined vise. Oh, man, it was *there;* she saw exactly what she wanted to do—

From nowhere, a scraping sound interrupted her concentration. A grating scrape, followed by a mysteriously soft *whoomph.* Her head shot up. Both sounds came from the outside, but definitely close enough to the house to be unignorable. Someone was on her property. In her driveway.

She heard the sharp, grating scrape again—what on earth *was* it?—followed by...damn...a wild baritone singing some kind of insane aria. A Russian aria.

She thought, *no.*

Perching up on tiptoe, she scowled out the window, but couldn't see anything or anyone from that view. The scrape-*whoomph* sequence repeated itself again, though. She pushed up her sweatshirt sleeves and stomped down the hall to the next bedroom. From that window, if she craned her neck far enough, she could see a bucketful of snow flying in the air, the sil ver shine of a snow shovel and, yeah, a disheveled head of coal black hair.

She thought, I'm gonna kill him. And headed for the back door to do just that. An occasional visit, fine. Stefan was alone in a new country and lonesome to talk with someone. Fine. He needed help with his language before he was safe to let loose in public—at least around women—and that was fine, too. She personally knew what it felt like to be a misfit, and she really didn't mind helping him.

Only the kiss last night had changed things.

She'd spent a sleepless night with Mr. Michaelovich barging into her dreams. Those dreams had been embarrassingly, explicitly sexual, brought on—no doubt—by her celibate life-style. Only no guy had bugged her dreams before Stefan. And neither had any other guy's kisses.

No one could help what they dreamed, but by George, a woman could control who used her snow shovel.

Bristling from every feminine nerve, she yanked open the back door—and almost earned herself a scoop of snow directly in the face. Thankfully the white powder frosted the overgrown yews next to the door—and by then Stefan had spotted her.

He leaned an elbow on the shovel handle and grinned. It *had* snowed the night before, four fresh inches of sugar-white powder adding to the foot-deep ground cover. Pine branches sagged under the weight; the naked hardwoods looked as if they were coated with a layer of whipped cream. The whole world had turned white except for one slam of color—him.

His cheeks were redder than apples; his eyes a dancing black. Backdropped against all that stark white, his shoulders looked huge and powerful—a wincing jolt of virile, vital masculine energy in a day that *had* been so serene, so calm, so peaceful.

"Good morning, my cupcake! You take my breath, you are that sexy this fresh in the morning!"

Paige wiped a hand over her face. Heaven knew what she looked like, but for positive it wasn't sexy, and he was not going to do this to her again. She was *not* disarmed by the way his Russian accent wrapped around that antiquated sexist endearment; she was *not* charmed by the totally unpredictable uses of the language that came out of his mouth. She was aggravated with him for this intrusion. Justifiably aggravated. But the damn man was so exuberantly enthusiastic, so *happy,* that yelling at him was harder than kicking a puppy.

"Good morning," she said, echoing him, her tone as formal as she could make it, and then forged ahead, "Stefan, there was absolutely no need for you to come over and shovel my walk!"

"Well, big confession to tell. Guilty confession." Stefan cocked an elbow on the shovel handle. "I not do this for you. I do this for me."

"I—pardon me?"

"I work on computer for hours. Very quiet, very silent work. Requires total focus. And this is my work, what I love, no question, but I get desperate for exercise. I have to break in—"

"Break out." She automatically corrected him.

"Yeah, you understand. Need to break out. I get energy buildup like to burst. I see you have no man, that it snowed last night, very easy for me to shovel your walk for you. Big favor to me, because I am so desperate to vent all this physical energy. I thank you for providing this chore.''

She opened her mouth. Closed it. She scalped a hand through her hair, feeling confused. So far she had yet to anticipate anything the confounded man was going to say. Ignoring the comment about ''no man'' was easy, but how was she going to argue with a guy who regarded snow shoveling as a personal favor to him?

And those dancing dark eyes mirrored utter sincerity. ''I found shovel by your back door. Easy to find. No reason to ask you, I know, because we are neighbors, and like you told me, it is natural for neighbors to help each other in America.''

''Well, I know I said that....'' Geezle beezle, talk about getting trapped by her own words. ''But this is a little different, Stefan. It scared me, when I heard an unfamiliar sound outside. I didn't know it was you—''

''Da, I can imagine. You live alone, any stranger could bother you. Not good, this danger, but I will watch over you now, Paige, no need to worry. And I tell you next time I'm here, so you know it's just me.''

Alarm shot through her. It was funny, really, even sweet that he thought she needed protecting—considering that no man, from the day she was born, had ever doubted that Paige could take care of herself. Her dad used to fret that she took self-reliance to a fault and tease that she was stubborn enough to take on a battalion of marines—but she'd never lacked the courage to stand up for herself. Maybe Stefan had grown up with some outmoded chivalrous values about women, though. And she didn't want to hurt his feelings, but somehow she was failing to communicate the concept of privacy.

"Stefan, it's okay—I'm okay—and I really don't need watching over. I can shovel my own walk, fix my own leaky faucets. I've been taking care of myself for a long time, and I've known everyone who lives in Walnut Woods all my life. The same families have been here for generations, and I..."

Her voice trailed off. Stefan was shaking his head before she halfway finished explaining. Something was on his mind, because he obviously wasn't listening to her.

"We talk another time, lambchop, because I can see you shaking. Too cold, standing there with no coat. You go back in. I not interrupt your work. You just pretend I'm not here, okeydoke?"

She ended up returning that "okeydoke," because it seemed to be the only word she was positive he understood. Pretending he wasn't there also struck her as a fine idea...until she tried putting it into commission.

The piece of coral was waiting for her. She couldn't be more excited about working on it. If she didn't exactly want Stefan around, at least she knew where he was. Outside. Lustily singing Russian opera in an off-key baritone. Clearly happy, and nowhere near her workroom.

When the singing stopped, she tensed for a second, then relaxed. He was done. Now he would surely go home. Naturally it had been difficult to relax, knowing he was so close, but now she could seriously concentrate.

And the silence and peace were wonderful, until she caught the whiff of spices in the air. Basil and ginger.

Pepper. And something hot and sweet and fruity—orange marmalade?

If forced at knife point, Paige could cook from scratch. Baking bread in the old wood stove was even a challenge she enjoyed, but day by day she leaned more toward throwing Lean Cuisine in the microwave. Frozen meals did the job better, and cooking for one was beyond boring. More to the immediate point, there could not conceivably be mouth-watering exotic smells emanating from the kitchen, because she hadn't *been* in the kitchen.

She found him standing over her wok, holding her fork, and her kitchen towel hanging from the belt loop on his jeans. Steam rose from the wok. Fragrant steam that smelled like something to die for. She crossed her arms, tapped her foot and delivered a cough from the doorway.

His head pivoted around, shaggy eyebrows arched in surprise. "You should be working."

"I was trying to," she said dryly.

"Well, this is a little lunch. A thank-you for letting me shovel your walk. I figure you are busy, too busy to maybe cook, so busy maybe you forget to eat. And I have all this—"

"You have all this energy. Yes, you told me. Energy enough to burst."

"I leave. Instantly. Soon as finished here." He waved a hand to illustrate his luncheon menu, which rivaled something she'd be lucky to put together for her family for Christmas. "I wanted to make you borscht, *blinchikis,* maybe *vatrushkas.* Give you samples of some Russian food. But couldn't find ingredients. Best I could do was Oriental. You probably hate Oriental, huh?"

"Oh, no, I'm crazy about Oriental food, but Stefan—"

"Great." He made an effusive gesture, shooing her out. "You go back to workroom. I'll bring in. Quiet as rat. Not bother you."

"Quiet as a mouse." She automatically corrected him.

"That's me," he agreed.

For a man who made ardent, extravagant and passionate protests about not bothering her, Stefan had managed to embed himself into her life as tenaciously as a tick on a hound.

Four days later, he showed up at her workroom door, carrying a tray. Paige took one look at the lunch of shiitake mushrooms and shrimp, and thought this had gone too far. Way too far. She had no idea where he'd found the oyster sauce or fresh cilantro leaves— certainly not in her kitchen. Completely without permission, Stefan had stacked her wood and stocked her kitchen and done all kinds of nefarious other chores over the past few days.

Someone was going to arrest him for B and E and Trespass unless he gained a grasp of American laws about privacy—and soon. Since polite tact hadn't gotten through to him worth spit, Paige figured that it was past time that she tried getting serious and tough with him. And she would.

But not until this lunch was over.

"Too much garlic?" Arms loosely crossing his chest, Stefan watched her bring the fork to her mouth and swallow the first morsel.

"The proportion of garlic is beyond perfect."

"Too many of the scallions?"

She refused to answer until she'd savored another bite. Maybe she was suspicious of him. Maybe she hadn't figured him out yet; maybe she was wary of what he wanted from her. But that man had a technique with a wok that could sweep any woman away.

Personally Paige had never indulged in any waste-of-time seduction fantasies about being swept away. The entire subject of sex was better buttonholed in a mental attic. But sex was sex, and food...oh, man, real food was her downfall. Decadence had never been this tempting. The delicate flavor of the mushrooms blended perfectly with the oyster sauce and soy and black pepper, giving the taste buds on her tongue a lust attack, and as for the sassy bite of cilantro...she swallowed. Unwillingly. "This is heaven. This is nectar. This is beyond to die for," she told Stefan. "Darned if I know why you're wasting your life as a physicist. You could make a fortune as a chef."

"To die for—this is good term?"

"The highest praise I know." She waved a fork at him—after taking another bite. "But you mustn't do this again. I mean it, Stefan." She gobbled another mouthful. "You've been helpful and wonderful, but you're taking the American concept of neighborliness too far. I can't take favors from you like this. It isn't right. It's making me uncomfortable. I really want you to stop, okay?"

Stefan watched another greedy forkful disappear into her mouth faster than a jet takeoff. "That's a straight high-five okeydoke no-sweat gotcha, lamb-chop."

Paige would have rolled her eyes—if she dared take her gaze off him. His command of the language was growing by leaps and bounds, thanks to the amount of time they'd spent together. He *did* relish every ounce of slang he picked up, but sexist slips like "lambchop" were happening less and less.

The problem in spending time with him, though, was her growing suspicion that Mr. Stefan Michaelovich was not really having all that much trouble with the language. It was mighty amazing that he grasped complex concepts faster than a finger snap, yet managed to misunderstand only when it mightily conveniently suited him.

The man had a teensy tendency to ignore—if not bulldoze—any obstacles in his path. Paige was becoming increasingly wary of his irresistibly innocent boyish shrugs and the "So sorry, I didn't understand." Stefan was innocent as she was genetic kin to a duck. But he hadn't tried kissing her again. Hadn't done one thing, in fact, beyond show up with frightening regularity—ánd usually after having done something nice for her out of the blue.

No one had ever spoiled Paige, and she'd never met anyone who indulged in random acts of kindness. It wasn't normal. It wasn't natural.

He *had* to want something from her, and Paige felt increasingly aggravated—and worried—that she couldn't figure out what it was.

She kept a suspicious eye on him while she finished lunch. He hadn't been in her workshop since that first morning with the fire, and he was investigating every nook and cranny and shelf more thoroughly than an FBI agent. His hands were slugged in the pockets of a brand-new pair of acid-washed jeans, his shoulders hunched in a No Fear sweatshirt. With the wild beard and unruly hair, he looked like an all-American motorcycle gang thug, like the bad-boy every mother warned her daughter about.

Like a man Paige should have the good sense to be scared of.

It was the first time her absentmindedness had struck her as a dangerous character flaw. She *meant* to remember that there were things about him that should logically scare her, but Stefan was so darned fascinating that worry kept slipping her mind. As he loped around the room, he fired a continual round of questions at her. She gave him the names for everything he asked—dop sticks, diamond wax, riffler, scorpers, gravers. Heaven knew why he asked. Her cameo-carving stuff had to bore any outsider witless. Yet typically, nothing escaped his curiosity and he took in every new vocabulary word as if he were a sieve.

"Stefan..." Finally she pushed aside her empty plate. "You haven't brought up your cousins since the first week you were here. How're they doing?" He'd mentioned his relatives in town, and she even vaguely knew the family; the couple ran a catering business. Yet as far as she could tell, he hadn't spent any time with them—much less in proportion to the time he was spending with her.

"They're fine. Good people, my kin. But right now they are gone to spend a month in Florida."

"Florida, huh?" She tried to sound interested rather than startled, but it never occurred to her that his only relatives had deserted ship, not when he was brand-new to a whole different country and way of life. He really was alone.

Except for her.

He flashed her a grin as he continued to roam around her shop. "My cousins told me ahead they had these travel plans. I figured out that this Florida trip is a major American must—rush south in the winter, hit the beach. The city I lived in, Petersburg, had reputation for the worst climate on planet. Torrential rains, endless fog, harsh and bitter winds. Beach is nice, but this cold climate is more what I am used to." He turned his head. "Is this the cameo you're making for your sister?"

"Yes. I hope. It's too soon to know if it's going to work out." She watched him bend over the leather-lined vise, where she had clamped the piece of coral. It couldn't look like anything to him. It wasn't anything yet. She'd determined the size, marked the outline with India ink, removed the back of the shell with a high-speed blade and lubricated the cut with water. Now it was back in the vise, waiting.

"There is frustration in your voice. You're having trouble with this?"

"Not...trouble. But I was lucky to find this piece—two-shaded coral is really rare." She didn't really know how to explain. "Every stone or shell is different. It has its own beauty, its own truth, nothing the artist can put in there, but something I have to find. That probably sounds weird—"

"Not weird," he said firmly.

"Well . . . anyway, coral is an especially fragile material to work with. Very easy to ruin with one wrong cut. And sometimes I have to study the raw material for a long time before I'm sure what to do with it." She motioned around the shop, where there were various cameos in different stages. "Each part in the process takes some studying and thought, so that's partly why I work on several pieces at the same time."

"I see. I also see many pieces that you have finished." He paused at the top shelf where she had a dozen finished cameos, ranging from pendants and jewelry to freestanding sculptures. "Paige?"

"What?"

"They steal my breath. And I am not making joke." His head swiveled toward her, eyes dark and piercing. "You create beauty like I have never seen."

She'd just taken a sip of hot Japanese green tea, tangy, almost bitter, and for a second she couldn't seem to swallow. Others had praised her work. Obviously she couldn't make a living at it if she were pit-awful rotten. Talent was an ingredient that enabled her to do something she loved, but otherwise she couldn't care less what anyone thought of it.

Yet his praise meant something. It was embarrassing, to feel the nest of warm fuzzies in the pit of her stomach, the sudden flush climb her cheeks. He wasn't even smiling, but he'd delivered that comment bare, in a quiet, rough-wrapped baritone that struck her as intimate and honest, meant to touch her. And it did.

"I'm not due that credit," she said quietly. "I don't really create, Stefan. All I can ever do is have the skill to bring out the best from the raw material."

"You take no credit for being creator? Whoever told you that was dimwit numskull, not appreciate you, sold you bucket of malarky." Numskull and malarky had been two slang expressions he'd picked up this week, and he'd been testing them in some mighty funny applications. Just then, though, there was no humor in his eyes or his voice. The frown on his brow was a scolding. "You have a gift for beauty, a gift for truth. It is everywhere in this room. Perfect example, this one—"

He strode over to the jade, the cameo of the woman staring at her reflection in the pond, the unsettling cameo that she'd made for her sister and had yet to figure out what to do with. Paige was surprised he'd even noticed it. It wasn't with the other finished pieces, but stashed in limbo by itself on another shelf. There was no specific reason she should have minded his seeing it, yet her pulse was suddenly beating uneasily, her nerves on some strange edge.

"This is you," he said.

"Pardon?"

"This is you, in the cameo." He glanced at her face, and his shaggy eyebrows suddenly arched in question. "Surely you knew this? That you captured yourself?"

That strange, sudden uneasiness instantly passed, as she let out a peal of laughter. "You have a wonderful imagination. That's nothing remotely like me, not in a million years. And that isn't how cameo carving works, Stefan. You can't do a portrait of yourself—or anyone else—nothing that deliberate. The carver works with the grain and layer of the stone, finds a face or profile in the raw material, but you can't ever 'order' that raw material to make a face you want."

"I understand this explaining. And not to get your liver in an uproar, my lambchop. I believe you." He motioned again to the jade. "But that's still you."

Four

"**D**o you need some money? You wouldn't be a doofus and lie if you needed some financial help, would you...? Yeah, I know you can take care of yourself, Gwen, but I've been making so much money I'm ashamed, downright sinfully ashamed—you'd be doing me a big favor if you took some of this guilty loot off my hands...okay, okay, don't get your pride all bent out of shape. I hear you, you're okay financially..."

Paige had grabbed the telephone just as she was climbing upstairs to get ready for bed. In one swift move, she lifted the receiver, tugged the mens' extra large Harvard nightshirt over her head and plastered the traveling phone to her ear again. She flicked off the bathroom light, then the hall light, still talking to her sister as she walked barefoot in the dark toward her bedroom.

"Well listen, Gwen, how about if I just send a plane ticket for you and my favorite monsters? You could just stay here for a couple of weeks, a month, rest up, give me a chance to spoil my nephews to death and get your mind off that son of a mangy cow...all right, all right, I won't call him a bastard or a sad excuse for a dust bag. You want to still think your ex as a nice guy, I'll pretend along with you. Hey, I'm on your team. But just so you know, if I meet up with him in person again, I'm gonna stomp his handsome face from here to Poughkeepsie—"

Her hand groped blind for the light switch in her bedroom. The overlight suddenly glared, illuminating the cherry four poster bed with the patchwork quilt, the Federal rocker, the marble-topped dresser with messily, gaping open drawers—which, she noted, no housekeeping fairy had come up and closed since morning. Her eyes honed faster than lightning, though, on the jade cameo on the dresser top, and suddenly her heart was skating faster than a toboggan down a steep hill.

She'd brought the cameo up here after lunch with Stefan. She didn't know why, didn't care why. It was her work, her art, and if she wanted to keep something private and out of sight, it was certainly her business.

Just for an instant, her gaze glued on the sensual profile of the woman in jade—and then faster than a slammed door, she flicked off the overhead light. It didn't matter if the room was pitch-black. All she was going to do was unbraid her hair and get ready for bed while she talked to her sister, chores she could do in a cave.

"...so tell me how the boys are doing. Raising hell, I hope...hmm...listen, kiddo, you know that if anything were wrong, all you'd have to do is tell either Abby and me, and we'd be there in thirty seconds flat? I know, you keep telling me you're doing fine, but I can't remember ever hearing this much stress in your voice..."

Paige tripped on something on the floor—probably a shoe—fumbled on the nightside table for her brush, and negotiated the perilous condition of her room in the dark. Curling up in the window seat, she loosened the rubber band—which pinged somewhere in space—then used her fingers to unplait the long braid.

"I do *not* work too hard. Geesh, how did this conversation get turned on *me?* Of course, I'm remembering to eat. And of course, I opened the bills and remembered to pay every single one of them this month." She had to quit unplaiting long enough to cross her fingers. "Sex? What's that? Oh. Yeah. Nope, haven't done anything like that...although, hoboy, you remember when we were kids, the three of us poring over that book by flashlight, terrified Dad was gonna catch us? Remember our deciding we all must be adopted? Because we knew for sure Mom and Dad would *never* do anything that disgusting..."

There. She'd made her sister laugh, and before they severed the phone connection, Paige felt relieved that she'd left Gwen in an upbeat frame of mind. They'd talk again in a couple of days—a week never passed before she talked with both her sisters. Gwen refused to admit that anything serious was bothering her, a frustration to Paige—she knew damn well something was. Eventually she'd worm the problem out of her sister, and in the meantime, Ma Bell kept them close.

Swiftly she finished unplaiting her hair, then shook it loose and free as she gazed out the window. It was magical outside, serene and still, the snow like a blanket of diamonds by starlight. It was a night for girlish dreams of princes and white knights... if Paige had been one to believe in fairy tales.

As she rhythmically brushed through the tangled strands, her hair shimmered and fell, tickling her nape, drifting down her shoulders and back. Somehow the texture of her hair invoked sensual, feminine feelings... yearnings... that never seemed to trouble her by day. It was only at night, that her four poster bed looked big and lonely. Only at night, that she would sometimes wake up from dreams, always alone, conscious that she had no one to wrap her arms around after a nightmare.

She still had nightmares, from that time in her life when she'd been spring-green young and wild—and a keg of dynamite hormones. She wasn't afraid of sex, she'd reassured herself a million times. In this small town, there were simply very few single men her age running around. Before that, she'd been busy learning her trade—and since the nature of her work was isolating, and she loved her work, a celibate life-style had just sort of... happened. Possibly she'd turned down a few opportunities, maybe even more than a few. But anyone who accused her of being afraid of intimacy or sex would be dead wrong.

An image of Stefan flashed through her mind. The brawny tilt to his shoulders, the wicked spark of sexual awareness in his eyes, the twist of a man's smile... a man's way of looking at her

For two weeks now, she'd convinced herself she was
imagining that look in his eyes. Clearly Stefan wanted
and needed a friend. He was lonely in a strange country, and that one kiss had simply been accidental—his
whole nature was physical and affectionate and exuberantly effusive. He didn't want her. She had no reason on earth to think he sought her company because
he *desired* her, and she'd never done one thing with her
appearance or actions to lead him in that direction.

Suddenly, though, she realized she was shivering.

Sitting on a window seat next to frostbite-cold panes
of glass, it was hardly a wonder the chill was getting
to her. She dropped the brush, bounced down and
dived straight for the cave of comforters and quilts.

Even in the dark, though, she could see the soft
glow of the jade cameo from the moonlight's reflection. Until she punched the pillow, turned the other
way and firmly closed her eyes.

As soon as Paige opened the door, Stefan thrust the
bowl in her hands. "I just want to bring you small
present, for being so kind about letting me use your
television. It's a sweet, called Russian Cream. We call
it 'food for the gods,' made of cream and sugar and
sour cream—nothing good for you, make arteries
cringe in horror—but believe you will find it one of
those to-die-for things."

"Stefan, you didn't have to do this." But he saw the
way she stared at the confection.

"Not *have* to, no. But I am much grateful that you
have dish antenna since my house does not. Cannot
get *Star Trek,* no way, on my plain old boob tube. And
almost late today. It's nearly four."

"I know. And, um, Stefan, I know I'm the one who introduced you to the show a couple of weeks ago, but do you think there's a teensy chance you've become obsessed with *Star Trek?*"

"Obsessed? Great word. You betcha, I am happily obsessed, would be devastated if I missed this two-parter with Spock." Casual and easy, he pushed off his boots and threw his jacket over a chair. Familiar with her house now, he copped a spoon from the kitchen, then aimed for her back den—and the remote control. The picture zoomed on the screen just as Kirk was explaining the *Enterprise* mission about going where no man has gone before.

A fitting analogy for Paige, Stefan increasingly suspected—and was conscious of her following him as far as the doorway, still holding the bowl of Russian Cream.

She had accurately guessed that he had a problem with obsession, although so far, she seemed to think a daily dose of rerun *Star Treks* was the cause. He was here for Paige, not Spock. And the way to her heart was clearly through her stomach, hence his bringing the Russian Cream.

His feelings for her had grown out of control, but as Stefan saw it, that problem was entirely her fault. He was lonesome for a woman, he knew that, but until knowing Paige he had no concept that he was not lonesome for any woman. Just her. Her grace, her eyes, her swift mind, her fanny, her humor, her endearingly absentminded ways—there was nothing about her that didn't draw him. The more he was with her, it was as if a key had unlocked feelings that he'd buried for years, deep inside him.

Paige wasn't immune to him. Even a single kiss had ignited lightning, a heat that simmered like a banked fire whenever they were in the same room together. She could not have missed it, and of course he had noticed her wariness around him. To a point he understood it. No civilized rules had ever obliterated primitive instincts, not where men and women were concerned. The hunt-and-chase of a courtship always aroused wariness in a woman; how could she know if a strange man was a predator seeking prey?

But he was not a wolf, seeking to conquer. He was just a man, seeking to love. And he'd hoped that time together—and his behaving himself—would naturally build her trust level with him.

It wasn't working. If anything, his lady seemed more tense around him instead of less. Helping him was different; Paige was a giver. She willingly accepted his company when she believed he needed help with the language, but Stefan was unsure how long he could pull off the bumbling-Russian-with-the-language routine.

In his work, he approached any impossible physics problem with patience, perseverance, and the process of elimination. There could be other reasons for her reserve. Doubts or concerns about his background, for one. And that was something he was hoping to bring up and deal with . . . today, if he could.

Paige was still hovering in the doorway. "You'll be okay alone? Because I really have to work."

"I know you do—you just go right ahead, lambchop. I am fine by myself," Stefan said easily. Having given permission for her to desert him had worked before, as it did now, to guarantee she would linger a little longer. She felt guilty about leaving him alone, was never quite sure what the etiquette of the situation should be. And by three minutes into the show, invariably her attention was caught.

It took four minutes, this time, before she perched on the arm of the old leather sofa. Four minutes after that, she'd fallen off that stiff wagon and was hogging her full half of the couch, sitting Indian-style with her legs crossed. He hadn't taken the spoon from the kitchen for nothing. Once he handed it to her, she leveled scoopfuls of the sweet faster than a kitten who'd been starved of food for a year.

"I have to get back to work," she muttered.

"I know you do."

"I don't even like the old Kirk and Spock episodes half as much as the new version. I just like Picard and Deanna and Data and Worf. Worf is so adorable."

Thanks to Paige's dish antenna bringing in countless channels, he'd seen both versions. "Worf, the monster you like? The prehistorical male chauvinistic caveman? What happened to the lessons on American feminism and sexist behavior and women's rights and—"

She gestured with the spoon, shushing him irritably. "There's a place for realism and a place for fantasy. This is fantasy. I'd probably never marry a guy like Worf in real life, but that doesn't mean I can't love him on screen."

"Ah. Is this example of American feminine logic?"

"Stefan?"

"Yes?"

"This Russian Cream is better than sin. I'm probably going to make myself ill, pigging out, because it is not possible to resist. I don't want you to think I'm not grateful. But I'm warning you, if you keep teasing me, I'm probably going to bop you over the head with a pillow."

If she'd chosen to bop him, Stefan noted there were dozens of pillows around. The small den was paneled in pecan, so small there was only space for the television, the couch, a lamp table, and a half-dozen tapestry pillows. There was some extremely interesting tickle-fight potential if she followed through with that threat, but somehow he didn't think she was quite ready for a tickle or a pillow fight. "Well, now you have me scared. I am shooking in my boots."

"Shaking, not shooking." She gently corrected him.

He already knew that. The more mistakes he invented in his speech, though, the easier Paige believed that he really needed her. The need was real enough. It just had nothing to do with language.

On the screen, Kirk ordered desperately, "Beam me up, Scotty." And then, at a crisis point, the monitor flashed to a feminine hygiene commercial. On daytime TV, the commercials were relentlessly dominated by diapers, laundry soaps and feminine hygiene. Stefan had seen them all, and so far hadn't learned one thing he didn't know.

About Paige, though, he hadn't even started learning. Not what he wanted to know. Not what he needed to know.

She was wearing gray sweats today, the sweatshirt oversize, the bottoms baggy. Even considering the practicality of such clothes to work in, Stefan thought she had a gift for choosing sexless attire—which was terrific, as far as he was concerned. Other men, he hoped, might not be tempted to look too close. When she leaned forward to set down the bowl, the graceful arch of her spine and the ripe fullness of her breasts trapped his attention like a rat in a cage. Much, much better, that she dressed demure.

She licked a last drop of the Russian Cream from her finger. If she did it again, he was probably going to sweat. "You're really getting bad, you know," she teased him.

"Me? Bad?" He'd been a monk. He hadn't done one thing.

She wagged a finger at him—the one that was still damp from the lap of her pink tongue. "You're really addicted to your daily dose of *Star Trek* reruns. You haven't missed one since you saw the first show."

Well, he'd been hoping for an opening to talk about certain things with her, and this couldn't get much better. "Actually there is a reason I am enamored of Spock. Watching is not just play, not just wasting time. I think Spock would understand the conflicts with loyalty I have been through. As you can. It is not so easy to find other people who have this understanding."

"Conflicts with loyalty?" She cocked her head. "What do you mean?"

He struggled to explain. "Your work is about beauty. The beauty you create speaks in a language every man knows, does not matter if he is from Asia or South America or Europe or anywhere else. Art is universal by its nature. And in that sense, you must be true to what you are trying to create—you have a loyalty to your work that just has nothing to do with the country you come from, yes? Would you not be unhappy if your work was locked up in a place where only a few could see it?"

"I never thought about using the word loyalty in that context," she said slowly, "but for sure, the answer is yes. Any artist has to be true to his craft—how else could anyone create anything honest or universal? And it would make no sense to create a piece of art that was locked up in someone's closet. But Stefan, I can't imagine how any of that could possibly relate to *Star Trek* and Spock—''

"So I explain. Spock was a Vulcan, started out loyal to his Vulcan heritage, but ultimately he was stuck with a bigger loyalty. I watch. Loyalty is always conflict for him. It is never his choice to reject his heritage, but is always the same—he must be true to the bigger principles that matter to him, the goals of the Starship *Enterprise,* principles of peace, of exploring other cultures without causing them harm.''

She shifted, swinging her legs under her, obviously taken with this idea. "Okay. I get what you're saying, about people having different kinds of loyalties— people like artists. And like Spock. But what that has to do with you—?''

Bottom-line time. Stefan took a breath. "I was born Russian, raised to be loyal to my country, and I felt much conflict and sadness when I left. Would be much easier to be a bus driver. But I am a physicist. I am stuck with certain abilities, certain talents. One day scientists will find a cure for cancer. Should their loyalty be to their country, or to the world? Physicists work on energy problems. Should their loyalty be to one flag, if answers to energy problem should affect whole planet, whole world, all nations? Your art, Paige, could not reach people if it was locked up in a vault. The problems I deal with in physics have power to affect people, too, just in different way.''

He had her full concentration now. He wondered if she realized that she'd naturally tucked closer to him.

Star Trek had been back on for several minutes. She'd forgotten it. Her attention was solely on him, her eyes as soft as the brush of brown velvet on his face. "You're not telling me this because you love to discuss philosophy, are you ... somehow I think there is another reason you brought all this up."

"Da. Yes, there is. It troubles me that you might think I am a disloyal man, a man of no commitment. I would not have you believe I left my country easily, as if I didn't give a damn. I gave a damn, lambchop. But I just could not live with my hands tied. I worked hard to find answers, then control over what happened to those answers was taken away from me. I never came to America to—how you say it?—freeload. I hope to contribute, to give back. But I must live where I have the freedom, the right, to share what I know, solutions, problems, with people everywhere. It is bigger loyalty that I am stuck with, do you understand?"

"Yes. I understand." Her eyes turned softer than any caress. "And I can understand how this must have been a very hard conflict for you to live with and resolve."

He studied her face. She *did* seem to understand, and her acceptance was a rich, soothing balm for his tired soul.

Still, he felt some confusion. She showed no sign that anything he'd said had startled or surprised her. He'd been half sure that her wariness around him was caused by believing he must be a ship deserter, a man who flew the coop on his country on a whim, a man of no commitment or loyalties. In her shoes, he would not have trusted or respected such a man.

Scotty beamed up Kirk yet again. Another commercial flashed on about hair color. The late afternoon light had grown darker, shadowing the room in a soft veil of gray. The furnace thundered on, rumbling a vague shudder through the house, making the radiators clank. In that closed-in space, he could smell old leather and dust, the drift of cinnamon and vanilla from a dish of leaves on the table, and more potent, the faintest spice and promise of a woman's perfume, a scent that was uniquely Paige.

Don't touch her. His conscience delivered the mental order, as if suddenly aware that choice was brewing in his mind. And yeah, it was. Brewing and cooking in his mind, and heating fast in his blood. He sensed it was a mistake to push Paige, sensed from their first meeting that it was her nature to bolt or rebel if she were pushed into anything.

But something changed in the spin of those seconds. One moment she was looking at him, her gaze thoughtful, her face laden with compassion as if she were still considering the conflict in loyalties he had to live with. The next moment she was still looking at him, still meeting his eyes, but she suddenly froze. Coral shot to those fine, delicate cheekbones. She swallowed. And her body tensed as if a poker had been welded on her backbone.

Maybe it had just now occurred to her how alone they were, how close they were sitting.

Maybe she had just now noticed that there was enough combustible chemistry between them to, no sweat, fuel a couple of starships.

And if she'd moved right then, Stefan might have talked himself into behaving. If she'd shown him one sign that she was troubled by his background, he might have talked himself into backing off.

But she didn't move. At all. Not when he slowly leaned forward. Nor when he gently tilted her chin, upward, toward him.

Her eyes widened in that instant before his mouth came down, covering hers as completely and warmly as a blanket on a bed. She tasted like Russian Cream, but beneath that was a flavor of a far richer sweetness. He remembered kissing her the first time, knew now, immediately, why that memory had unshakably clung in his memory. Morning dew on a rosebud might taste like her, or liquid star shine, or the first crystal droplets of a fresh spring rain. Young. The taste of her was young, and made him feel as young as spring fever and as if the whole damn world were suddenly new.

Her lips, though, were locked tighter than a sealed vault. He wasn't absolutely sure if they'd take a crowbar to open.

Still, fear was hugely different from reluctance. Her hands were jammed in her lap, knuckles white, and she was so tense she could hardly breathe. He could not fathom how or why she would be afraid of him...but such a misconception simply had to be corrected.

He would not hurt her. This he explained with a series of tender kisses, explained with a feather-gentle caress that stroked from her cheek to her throat. Kisses from him, kisses in general, were nothing to be afraid of. It was wondrous, this connection between a man and a woman. Like nothing else. Better than nectar, better than moonlight, better than flying high on the wings of a summer day. It was private, this connection. A secret. The only kind of secret in the universe that one couldn't keep because it always, wonderfully, took two.

Her hands clutched his arm, her fingers biting as if they were the talons of a bird, then loosened, slowly. Slowly her hands climbed up his shoulders, roped around his neck. Slowly her eyes turned drowsy. Slowly that ready-to-bolt tension seeped out of her muscles... and suddenly, swiftly, wildly, she was kissing him back.

Stefan had never known a hundred women, never wanted to, could never see a purpose in playing where the stakes didn't matter. Satisfying sexual needs may have relieved frustration, but there was no real fun unless there was a serious potential for dynamite and danger, unless the woman made his blood spin.

She made his blood spin—faster than the fire tail on a comet. She might not have wanted to be kissed, but when she kissed back... she kissed back. His tongue dipped in the secret corners of her mouth, tasted, came back for more. Her throat arched for the pressure, yet she returned his openmouthed kiss with pressure of her own.

In a hundred ways, she had already shown him that she was a sensual, vulnerable woman. But he never anticipated an outpouring of emotion like this. Her long strong body bowed, leaning into his. She shivered, hard, when his hand slid from her side to cup a firm, full breast. She made a raw, soft sound as if he hurt her, when he could not have hurt her; his touch could not have been more reverent, more gentle, more cherishing.

It was as if she'd dammed up needs and feelings for a century, as if she'd never let them loose before. At his nape, her hands were kneading, kneading, the way a kitten so unconsciously expressed pleasure. He stroked down her long, supple body, feeling her flesh yield and warm through the heavyweight sweatshirt, feeling the sweet curve of her hip fill his palm as he dragged her over his lap.

Fire this hot could burn a man up, and he was already aroused harder than pain. Her fanny nestled where he hurt most, yet she would not sit still, her hands as restless as her mouth, stealing kisses faster than he could give them to her free. Their noses bumped. Her elbow stabbed his ribs. Her awkwardness and urgency moved him, inflamed him, as no skilled seductress ever could. He thought of the woman in her jade cameo, that striking and unforgettable image of both innocence and a natural rich, deep sensuality. Paige's response was fierce and frantic, as if she were just discovering gold and was afraid that dream would disappear in a puff of wind, a wrong breath, a beat of time.

He was not going to disappear.

He might burn up and explode, but positively he was not going to disappear.

She bucked away from him suddenly, lifting her head, her drowsy eyes suddenly bolting wide and huge. Beyond the cool crunchy sound of the incredibly uncomfortable leather couch, there'd been no sound, no change, nothing he knew that had startled her. But the blaze in her soft brown eyes was kin to fear, sick-sad fear, and shock. Just as quickly, her whole posture turned rigid.

"I don't know how this happened," she said desperately.

He had no idea how to soothe her, because he had no idea what she needed soothing from. He touched her cheek. "I kissed you, *lyubeesh*. You kissed me back. It's okay. I don't think this takes complicated analysis."

"But... I didn't mean to. We were just watching *Star Trek*..." She glanced wildly at the TV. *Star Trek* was long over. Men dressed very foolishly like gorillas had taken over the screen. Her eyes whipped back to his, still looking dazed and confused. "Stefan, I thought we were friends."

"I hope this, too. I hope this strongly."

"I didn't... I never... meant to lead you on."

"Lead me on?" It was a helluva time to have his knowledge of English fail him, and something about that phrase painted two flags of color on her cheeks.

"Lead you on means to tease you." She swallowed. "To make you think I was inviting a chance to sleep with you. To lead you to believe that. Unfairly."

That, he had no trouble understanding. Perhaps it was time to admit to a character flaw. "No one, lambchop, leads me anywhere. It is a problem I've had my whole life, that I listen to my own heart, my own conscience, and cannot seem to follow where anyone else is determined to so-called lead me." He grappled again for more words, since those didn't seem to be reassuring her worth carrots. "We neck, yes. But we did not get it on. We did not hit your sack. You still even have your socks on. No reason to be afraid, Paige."

"I'm not afraid," she said sharply.

Poker was no game for her; she was disastrous at fibbing. But he said gently, "I probably said wrong word. You know how bad I am with my struggling language. But I am relieved to hear that you're not afraid of me."

"I'm not," she said again.

"Good. Because we would have to discuss this fear, if that were so. I would not harm you, not do anything you did not want, not ever deliberately scare you. A man would do that, in my eyes, is frog."

As if suddenly realizing she was still on his lap, she scrabbled off quickly... but she also suddenly chuckled.

"I not mean anything funny," he said quietly.

"You didn't say anything funny. You just said something wonderful. I agree with you, any man who would force a woman is a low-down frog. But Stefan, I was not afraid you would do that."

Low-down. He mentally stored that term, sure he would use it again now that he knew it made her smile. Temporarily, though, there seemed no recovering from how uncomfortable she was with him. Deliberately he glanced at his watch. "Good grief, I didn't realize it was this late. I better go home, to work, and you must get back to work, too, lambchop."

"You couldn't be more right."

Stefan left, but his assessment of the situation was the total opposite. Nothing was right. Something very serious, in fact, seemed to be wrong. She'd come apart in his arms as if she were a lover born for him. That kinship of spirits was rare and precious, and he could not believe he had mistaken her response.

So she *was* afraid. Of something.

Somehow he had to find a way to uncover whatever it was.

Five

Paige locked herself in the workshop for an hour. Never mind that Stefan had totally broken her concentration. Until he'd come over—and sandblasted her entire afternoon—she'd been on a roll. Finally it had happened. A breakthrough.

Partially finished cameos were strewn all over the shop—projects in jet, tortoise shell, amber and mother-of-pearl—but they were coming fine. It was the coral cameo for her sister that had been giving her fits, and it was the one that mattered most to her.

She'd done all the base work. She'd already removed the rough backing, lubricated the first cuts with water, and carefully, painstakingly filed the exterior layers. The next step was the actual carving.

For two blasted weeks, she'd studied that coral upside and down, willing it to talk to her, frustrated that she could not see the truth in it, the vision, the potential picture.

But this morning, she'd picked up excitement. Squirm-in-her-seat, bounce-up-and-down excitement. Few things on earth required more rigid and exacting discipline than cameo carving, and Paige both demanded and expected that rigid discipline from herself. But when serious creative inspiration hit, her mood soared hopelessly into the stratosphere.

It had hit like a sniper's bullet, all at once. Suddenly she *saw* it. Two potential faces in the coral. Echoed in the two shadings of color, one rose, one paler—the profile of one woman shadowing another. And oh, man, that was so much like her sister, so perfect. Gwen's self-image was so different than the woman Paige knew her sister to be. Gwen never saw herself as beautiful, as wonderful and warm and giving and compassionate, the way her sisters saw her, the way *everyone* saw Gwen but Gwen.

And it was there in the coral.

Or it *had* been earlier in the day.

An hour later, Paige tossed down the graver in disgust, stomped around the shop slamming drawers and putting away tools. Concentration was her gift, her talent, her forte. She *never* had a problem with it. Ever.

Until That Man had come into her life.

Scowling, she trudged down the hall into the kitchen and yanked open the door to the refrigerator. Some absentminded nitwit had put the peanut butter and bread in the fridge after lunch. More to the point, the same nitwit had forgotten to defrost anything for dinner. She slammed the refrigerator door closed. She wasn't hungry anyway.

She stalked toward the stairs, figuring a nice long shower would shake her out of this restless mood. The phone rang when she was on the third step. She hesitated—no way she wanted to talk with anyone right then—but it could be Abby. Her oldest sister almost always called on Thursdays. The answering machine picked up after the second ring, but it was a man's mellow tenor on the line.

"Paige? It's me. I know you're there—I also know damn well you won't pick up if you're working—but just try not to erase the message this time, would you? I'm shooting you a big fat check in the mail, more than even I'd hoped for. You're temporarily rich, you crazy hermit. But I need to talk to you about orders ahead, and how soon you're going to be finished with what pieces. Just give me a ring in the next couple days. And write that *down,* Paige, so you don't forget."

Harry Sims. She could never mistake his voice. Harry was the only man in her life, and he was a godsend. She'd never wanted anything to do with the hoity toity art world. As far as she was concerned, cameo carving was no different from being a plumber. It was what she did. Her chosen work. And she just wanted to be left alone to do it in peace.

But Harry made that possible. She mailed him her work; he sold it. He did all the marketing and business, the art shows and art world nonsense. He'd found her ten years ago, tracked her down when he saw one of her cameos at a jeweler's in Boston. They'd been instantly compatible. The art world was his love, where she hated it, and Harry was gay—not that anyone would know that to look at or talk with him. But he respected her choice of solitude and anonymity, respected other people who were different, never made judgments or asked questions that were none of his business. Too many people had done that to him.

Her affection for Harry was real, but the message on the answering machine was forgotten as fast as she heard it. Just then, she had an entirely different man on her mind.

She pulled the sweatshirt over her head while she was still climbing the stairs, yanked off the rubber band holding her braid while she was stomping through the hall. In two minutes flat, she planned to be in a hot shower and washing that man right out of her hair like the song went.

There were reasons Stefan was seeping under her skin. It wasn't his Russian Cream. The damn man had an irresistible sneaky sense of humor; he'd made her laugh and he'd made her think, and he'd about torn out her heart when he talked about his conflict of loyalties. A man that hopelessly idealistic needed protecting. She'd been a rebel herself—but not like him. He sounded so alone. He sounded as if he'd always been stuck bucking the tide, to live how he believed. Men that good were rare and special, and yeah, Paige understood perfectly well why she was drawn to him.

It was the *other* part she didn't understand.

Her whole body felt shaky. Weird. Achy. Self-aware. She wasn't used to feeling desire, wasn't used to this pipe-bomb blast of stupid, rich, butter-soft... yearning. She had almost made love with him on the cracked leather couch in the den, and a no had never even crossed her mind. She wasn't used to a man turning her inside out. Physically or emotionally.

And it couldn't be allowed to happen again.

She flipped on the bedroom overhead light. No surprise, her gaze zoomed straight to the jade cameo on her dresser. And no surprise, her instinctive response to the woman in jade was an uneasy, unsettled edginess. The cameo was a beautiful piece of art, which was hunky-dory. But there was something about that woman that personified free, abandoned sensuality—and grated on Paige's nerves like a child's piercing cry.

There was nothing admirable about wanton behavior, nothing to respect in a woman who let her hormones run free. Paige wasn't "abandoned." She wasn't irresponsible. She had spent ten years building up inhibitions, and she wanted every one of them. Maybe once she'd been a selfish, careless teenager, but that was a bridge long down. She wanted to be exactly who she was now: a disciplined woman who knew damn well how to control inappropriate behavior. Or she had. Until this afternoon with Stefan.

Impatiently she tossed her sweatshirt over the jade cameo—covering it completely. And then flicked off the light and headed straight for the shower. She flipped the faucets on full blast, finished stripping down and stepped in. The hot water sluiced down her skin, soaking, steaming. She willed it to make these shaky, edgy feelings disappear.

Sometime, she wanted a family and children. That dream had never been off her table. She'd never planned a celibate life-style. There were times, whole long lonely nights, when she craved someone to love. And to be loved by.

It wasn't a *man* she was afraid of. But he had to be the right man. A professor or a teacher, maybe. Someone quiet, someone distracted and absorbed by work the way she was, someone she could talk with, someone she felt safe with when the lights went off at night.

A boisterous, effusive, gregarious and exuberantly sexual man...like Stefan. Holy kamoly. Whatever that irrepressible Russian did to turn her inside out ... this was all very simple. And her mind covered the entire discussion and analysis in a single word. *No.*

"Stefan, what on earth are you *doing?*"

Stefan looked up. It would seem pretty obvious what he was doing. Paige's house had an old-fashioned coal shute leading into the basement. The shute was no longer used for coal, but the opening was handy for throwing wood inside, and once he had her basement full of firewood, he'd started stacking it. Hot work. So hot that he'd naturally stripped off his flannel shirt or he would have been outright broiling.

All this, he thought, she was way bright enough to figure out without asking. On the other hand, she *did* look magnificent with her hands on her hips and her eyes blazing—a true Valkyrie. The warrior-woman effect was a teensy bit sabotaged by her floppy socks and pale pink sweatshirt, but Stefan sensed he'd better not risk a grin. "Well, lambchop, I needed to do something for you. I felt bad that I upset you yesterday."

"You did not upset me."

He let that little fib pass on by. "Well, I felt to blame. I felt buckets of guilt. I felt ... a good friend would not upset another friend. I did not want you to think I was a turkey." He noticed her hands slip from that aggressive posture on her hips. The word "turkey'"seemed to do it.

"For heaven's sakes, Stefan. I never thought you were a turkey."

"Well, in meantime, I see how fast your wood stove and fireplace are eating wood. Need more before winter is over. I cut wood for my house, easy enough to cut some for you, too. I have physical energy to burn, as I explained before, so you are doing me big favor by providing this chore." He paused. "I also think that hauling wood is not good for you. You could hurt your hands on work like this. You need your hands to make cameos."

"My hands are always a mess, Stefan. It wouldn't make any difference if I got another cut or a scrape."

His eyebrows arched in a disbelieving frown. "Either you have problem with vision or you have bolt loose in head. I have seen your hands many times. They are not a mess. They are strong, beautiful, exquisite hands."

"I..." Heaven knew what she started to say, but she abruptly swallowed it, and weakly fell back on correcting his language. "When you're trying to tell someone they're crazy, the term is screw loose, not bolt loose."

"Boy, good thing you explained that, toots, because I really had that confused. I could have sworn you told me the word 'screw' was not politically correct. I will remember next time that this is an exception when it's okay to screw. Good thing I have you to help me with my struggling language, huh?"

She sank onto the basement steps as if she were suddenly exhausted, and rubbed two fingers on her temples. He couldn't hold back a grin then. She seemed confounded by the direction the conversation had turned. And though he was increasingly challenged to keep up the bumbling-Russian-with-the-language routine, it was sure hard giving up something that worked so well.

Her eyes, he noticed, darted all over the basement from the dark cobwebbed corners to the woodpile to the pipes in the ceiling. Everywhere, but on his bare chest. He considered pulling on his flannel shirt, and then thought, no.

"Stefan," she said, "I don't think I'm up for explaining, but just forget the word 'screw' completely, okay? When you want to tell someone they're crazy, just tell them they're crazy."

"Okeydoke."

"In fact, it might be best not to tell anyone they're crazy. Even if they're plumb wacko. It's just sort of . . . rude."

"Okeydoke."

"And about your hauling and stacking all this wood for me—"

Stefan gently interrupted. "Actually we were talking about your wonderful help with my learning the language. I could not be more grateful. And I was wondering if you might try an outing with me. You know. In the real world."

"An outing?"

"Da. I was thinking about dinner. Taking you out."

"Stefan, I don't think—"

"The thing is, it is not obvious to me, the language mistakes I am making in public. If you were with me, you would see what I am doing and saying incorrectly. This is a huge imposition, I know. Maybe you would be embarrassed to be seen with a Russian immigrant who does not have cool language skills—"

Her head shot up. "It'd be a cold day in hell before I was embarrassed to be with a friend, Stefan."

It was so easy, he mused, to arouse her fiercely passionate nature—and her instinctive sense of loyalty toward those she cared for. How amazing, that she had yet to see how alike they were. The devil made him press just a little harder. "I would feel badly if I upset you again. It is okay. I would understand if you felt embarrassed about being with me—"

"That's absolutely ridiculous." She lurched to her feet. "I'd be proud to be with you, anytime, anywhere. We're going to dinner and that's that."

"Well . . . if you insist."

"I do."

"Okeydoke," he said genially. "Seven o'clock tonight then. I pick you up here. That sound like a peachy keen plan?"

"I . . . yes. I think. I . . ." She shook her head suddenly, as if trying to clear a fog from her mind. She did not seem very clear about who had just talked who into going to dinner. "I'm going back to work, Stefan."

"Good idea." He slapped the wood dust from his hands as he watched her swivel around and climb the stairs out of sight. The little swish in her fanny easily raised his body temperature ten degrees.

It was the look in her eyes, though, that aroused the temperature in his heart.

He had given up a great deal in his life. Work, friends, family, country—all to appease his sense of honor and what was right by his conscience. It didn't matter if those choices were easy or hard. When the lights were off, a man had to live with himself.

Still, he had never loved before—not a love from the gut. Not a love that defined loyalty and commitment to another person, beyond all other factors, beyond rhyme or reason. He was not there yet with Paige. But he intuited that he was on that cliff ledge, facing a risk he had never fathomed before. For so long, he had blindly believed there was nothing he couldn't sacrifice if he had to.

Not her. Even now, even this soon, he had the frightening, uneasy feeling that he would lose part of himself if he lost her. How to win her, though, how to discover her true feelings, struck him as the toughest battle he'd ever faced. And no outcome was assured.

Paige thumbed through the hangers in her closet. Jeans, jeans, shirt, jeans, overalls, shirt, shirt, dress…

Her fingers hesitated on the hanger, and then she yanked out the dress. It hadn't seen the light of day in a couple of years. Abby had given it to her. Abby had superb taste in clothes—which she told both sisters enough times to make their eyes cross.

As mercilessly as they teased Abby about being a clotheshorse, though, she invariably picked out stuff for her and Gwen that suited them. Doubtful Abby would be caught dead herself in a simple burgundy sweater dress that had no particular claim to an in-style or savoir faire. But it was comfortable. It fit like a worn-in old friend. It had long sleeves, turtleneck and was midcalf length. It covered everything.

Stefan had mentioned Palmer's, and the restaurant just wasn't a jeans place. A dress was simply more appropriate, and there wasn't a single reason not to wear it…other than a generic panic at the implications of going out on a date—and specifically a date with Stefan.

After fumbling for five minutes in her drawers, she finally found a slip and stockings. She pulled those on, then the dress, then chased into the bathroom before she lost her nerve. There was makeup in the bathroom. Abby had given her all those bottles and tubes, too—after lengthily ranting on about Paige being incapable of picking the right colors and makeup on her own.

She *could* have. She just hadn't. For a few more minutes, she scrabbled around with pots and tubes and mascara wands, then checked the mirror. She still had to braid her hair—it wasn't as if this was a finished product yet—but the reflection in the mirror still appalled her. The face paint looked great, but the damn fool woman in the mirror had helplessly, infuriatingly scared eyes. Paige wasn't afraid of a tornado, for Pete's sake, and she *never* ran from a problem. Never had, never would.

But damn. Wherever this disgusting coward streak was coming from, she needed some moral support from the Mounties.

As fast as she could pelt downstairs—carrying heels—she grabbed the phone and punched in her sister's number at work. As soon as she heard Abby's voice, she snapped, "Darn it, what am I supposed to wear for jewelry with this dress?"

Abby, thankfully, was notoriously efficient. She never had a problem picking up a conversation midstream. She answered as smoothly as if she'd been waiting for this precise question for months. "Gram's garnets, of course. The color's perfect. They're right in your left top drawer in a white box. Who is he?"

"A new neighbor. And don't ask. I'm not sure of this."

"I won't ask. But you either call me tomorrow or I'll shoot you. And Paige?"

"What?"

"Don't wear those stupid tan leather shoes. You've got some black ones up in the closet that'd look great. And there's Shalimar in the bathroom. Spray a little on."

"I was never going to wear the tan shoes." Paige instinctively tucked her hand behind her back—the one that was holding the tan shoes. "And this isn't a Shalimar type dinner. It's just a plain old ordinary dinner."

"Ah. Well, wear the Shalimar anyway. It'll make you feel good. You'll relax more if you feel good. And listen, you dimwit. Everything the militant feminists told us about guys is wrong. They're not the enemy. That whole half of the human species is definitely a little weird, a little alien, but the world'd be utterly tedious and boring without them. Take it easy. Don't get fretful. It's just a guy. Just a dinner."

"What is all this advice? I've never been *fretful* in my entire life...." She heard the sound of knuckles rapping on her front door. "Oh, God. He's here."

Her sister barely sneaked in a "Good luck" before Paige whisked the phone back onto the receiver and hustled to answer the door. It wasn't seven yet. It wasn't even a quarter till. She was still supposed to have plenty of time to do the earrings and hair and shoe stuff.

Yet she forgot all that the instant she saw him. There were reasons why she was worried about this dinner, but she forgot those, too. Stefan had trimmed his beard, had cut his hair. The topcoat was new, and so, she suspected, was the navy sport coat and slacks. The tie was navy and had a pattern of American flags on it, and was hanging askew, tied tight enough to strangle him. His black eyes skimmed over her face and figure faster than a cat could lick cream, but before she could say anything—before he even stepped in—he cleared his throat and confessed, "Paige, I am hugely nervous."

Her heart instinctively melted. All those schoolgirl nerves dissipated faster than smoke. She wasn't a schoolgirl. And he was a friend who needed her. "For heaven's sake, Stefan. You know me. No one's going on this dinner but us. What on earth is there to be nervous about?" As soon as he stepped in, she closed the door and aimed straight for his tie. It wasn't a matter of choosing to be physically close to him. He was going to choke on that tie if someone didn't fix it.

He lifted his chin so she could work. "I am not doing so well with my culture gap. I seem to have formed habit of saying wrong things in public situations. I look okay?" He immediately qualified that question. "I not want to look Russian. I want to look American. Fit in with the guys."

If he wanted to look like other men, he was always going to fail, she mused. But that wasn't because of his background. It was because of his incredible sexy black eyes and the devil's smile and a towering height that was always going to be damn hard to hide in a crowd. She stepped back to look him over. The tie was better. No matter how hard he'd brushed that hair, it was already starting to look disheveled, but the trimmed beard at least made him look a bit more tamed. A bit. "You look very American," she assured him. "And the tie is adorable. You spiff up extremely well, Michaelovich."

"Spiff up?"

"It means that when you dress up, you really look different—you shape up great, look really handsome."

"Ah. Well, you also spiff up, my lambchop. In fact, you steal my heart, you are so damn beautiful."

She certainly didn't believe that, but for an instant she couldn't seem to swallow. Positively the sweater dress wasn't tight or suggestive, but it definitely draped her figure differently than the kind of pouchy, poochy pair of sweats he usually saw her in. He noticed. She'd meant to put her hair up, not leave it loose and messy. He noticed the flowing sweep of her hair, too, and clearly approved. Legs, figure, hair, even the soft shine of her lip gloss...Stefan noticed. And the look in his eyes kindled every feminine nerve in her whole body.

Her tongue eventually moved. In fact, it started rattling as she spun around and aimed for her winter coat in the hall closet. "Really, there's nothing to be worried about. We're just going to have an easy dinner. Nothing's going to go wrong. I'll help you out, if you get in trouble with the language..."

She buttoned her camel coat, swung a scarf around her neck and joined him at the door.

"You are much reassuring me," he told her.

"Good. We'll have a great time, and that's that."

"I am in full agreement."

He might be in full agreement, but even though she'd reached his side, he seemed to have stopped dead—he made no move to open the door.

"What's wrong? Are you nervous about something else?"

"No, not worried about anything else, toots. I was just thinking, lots of snow outside. Might be best," he said tactfully, "if you wore shoes."

She looked down. Stocking feet. No shoes.

The chances of her surviving this evening, she figured, were about five million to one.

Six

"Now listen, Stefan, I know you use certain expressions with me, like lambchop and toots and babe. But that's different because I know you don't mean anything by them. You want to be careful not to use expressions like that around other women."

"Yes, Paige."

"And I know how much you like to try out your slang. And that's a great idea, because I can tell if you're using something wrong, and how else would you know unless you tested it?"

"Yes, Paige."

"But around other people, it would be better if you forgot, um, any sexual references you ever heard. I mean, like 'hit the sack.' Or 'I want to get it on with you.' No matter what your friend taught you, that just isn't the standard way a man talks to a woman around here."

"Yes, Paige. Um, Paige?"

"What?"

"I must confess that I find these rules confusing. It is clear that being able to talk about sex is important here. They use these phrases on TV shows, in ads, in the newspapers and magazines. I thought this was accepted practice. I thought it was required. In fact, I spent one whole day carefully watching daytime TV and—"

"Holy kamoly! You stay completely away from those soap operas, Stefan! The *last* thing you need to do is get any ideas about American real life from them."

"A big no-no, huh? Good thing I have you to ask these frank questions. How else could I learn?"

Well, that was just it, Paige thought glumly. He didn't seem to have anyone else to ask these questions. Left alone, God knew what assumptions he'd come up with about American culture, and she couldn't deny feeling increasingly protective of him.

She didn't deny the uncomfortable, disturbing feelings Stefan aroused in her, either, which was one of the prime reasons she had agreed to this dinner. Further time with him would surely help her sort out those strange emotions. She was an adult; she'd never run away from the truth. She wanted control over her feelings again; she wanted her natural, normal perspective back. Stefan needed a friend and she was determined to be one.

She didn't *feel* like a friend, though, when he ushered her into Palmer's with a possessive hand at the small of her back. The restaurant was a converted house from Revolutionary War times. There were a half-dozen rooms, all intimately small, each dominated by a stone-blackened fireplace and sooty-dark beams. No one else was seated in the room where the maître d' led her and Stefan. The tall skinny windows had velvet drapes swagged with tassels, the tables were covered with dark red damask, and the only source of light was the roaring fire and candlelit sconces.

A waitress in eighteenth century garb served them red wine and steaks on pewter platters. She was a darling, with peaches in her cheeks and huge, dark eyes, yet Paige noted that Stefan didn't call her lambchop or babe. During dinner, the chef made a customary visit to make sure they were happy, and two old friends paused in the doorway to say hello. She didn't hear a word of slang from Stefan either of those times.

She had cautioned him about his language, of course. But it still seemed amazing how quickly he dropped that tendency when he had such a hard time conquering those endearments with her. She had also never suspected that her uncivilized and unruly bear had the impeccable manners of a gentleman... except when he looked at her.

For some reason he paid no attention to the waitress—who was adorable. And he barely glanced at an old school friend, Mary Wilkins, when she stopped to chat—even though Mary was striking enough to turn any man's head. Stefan was only looking at her... as if the rest of the people in the world were a nuisance. As if he'd rather have had her for dinner instead of the T-bone. As if her face by candlelight was damn near mesmerizing.

Since that was poppycock, Paige decided the dim lighting was responsible for tricking her imagination. Either that, or the wine. By the time they'd finished dinner and the plates were cleared away, Stefan had refilled her glass twice now.

"You sure you don't want dessert, lambchop?"

There. She *knew* a lambchop would slip out sooner or later—but her mind was on another subject entirely by then. She was determined to get to know him better, determined that these incessant, unsettling sexual vibrations around Stefan would disappear if she just understood him better. And he was making that job so easy. They'd been talking as naturally as old friends. "No, honestly, I'm too full to try dessert. Tell me more about your growing up years. You were really taken away from your parents?"

"Not 'taken away' in a cruel sense. It was how education was done. Six days a week—and the school day so long that a child would have had to commute very late at night. It just made more sense to board at the school. And this was not automatic for everyone. I tested high in mathematics when I was very young, so I was put in an educational program suited especially for that."

"Well, that part sounds great. But I'd have died growing up without my mom and dad, without my sisters. My family was everything to me. Who patched your scratched knees? Taught you to ride a bike? Dosed you with medicine when you were sick?"

"There were all kinds of caretakers. They just weren't family."

"It sounds like a very lonely way to grow up," she said quietly.

"Da, that it was."

"Your mom and dad—they're still in Russia?"

"My mother caught pneumonia when I was twelve. The virus went out of control and we lost her. My dad, though, is still there." Stefan wrapped his palm around the wineglass. "I can't say that we are close. Many harsh words between us. He's . . . an emotional man. We are peas in the same pod. He cannot compromise what he believes. Nor can I. I recognize that we are the same, where he can only see where we are different."

Although the subject of his dad was obviously painful, Stefan had willingly brought it up. Paige groped, unsure how far he wanted to pursue it. "Was your dad . . . angry with you for coming here?"

"More than angry. I am not sure forgiveness from him will happen," he admitted shortly. "I am his only son. He sees me as a traitor."

"Oh, Stefan. No wonder you've had such an unlivable conflict of loyalties. You didn't even have support from the home front, did you?"

"I never expected support, but I'm sorry for both of us that he could not understand. I've written him. And will keep writing him. Some say that enough time can erode the hardest stone. Best I can do."

"You have plans? For what you want to do here?"

"Oh, yes." His shaggy eyebrows arched in surprise at the question. "I had definite plans long before I left Russia. Coming here was not difficult like before the Berlin Wall went down. Anyone can travel. But it is still no piece of cake to permanently leave. My American cousins gave me contacts, and the American Embassy went to bat for me. I would have had difficulty with visas, travel arrangements, all the legalities without help. There were Americans who helped me with this from the start. I want to teach."

Paige dropped her napkin. "A teacher? You want to be a *teacher?*"

Her startled expression produced an immediate response. "Paige, trust me, I am qualified. I have beyond Ph.D. education in mathematics and physics. And before I stepped foot on American soil, I had offers from three of your universities to—"

"Stefan, I wasn't doubting your qualifications. It's just going to take me a minute to, um, think of you as a teacher."

"This blow your mind in someway, *lyubeesh?*"

"No, no. I just . . ." She swallowed hard. Her mind wasn't blown, but it was definitely humorously spinning. For years, she'd envisioned a teacher-type as the only kind of man who would ever work for her—a nice, quiet academic type, someone who was driven by work, someone comfortably absentminded and not really emotional. Like her. And it wasn't that she thought all teachers fit that stereotype, but Stefan was boisterous and impulsive and sexy and as physical as a caveman. Sure, he could teach. But it was sort of like starting a dream with a nice, safe monk turn into a leather-jacketed motorcyclist. A definite mental adjustment. "Tell me more about your plans," she said swiftly.

"Well. Working for government, working on areas like weapons and security, is automatic consideration for someone with my educational background. I was steered relentlessly in this direction in Russia. For me, this is no good. It is against my heart. I will not. So even when help was first offered to me, I made clear— I am honest—that I will not work on weapons. I want to work with young people. I love kids." He paused. "You like kids?"

"Sure. How can anyone not be crazy about kids?"

"Da. I was sure you would feel that way." His dark eyes suddenly glowed on her face with the power of moonbeams, and was backed up with a huge smile. "In long run, there is more work than teaching that I need to pursue. For certain projects, I need connection with other physicists. For this, I need computer and modem, the ability to travel from time to time. This work is important to me, too, but children are the world's future, yes? So I see teaching as first priority."

"A teacher," she echoed again. Surely this was going to strike her as funny by tomorrow. The curious thing was that she really *could* see him as a teacher, easily imagine him controlling a class but also winning over urchins of any age with his big, boisterous affectionate ways and humor. Kids sensed when they could trust an adult. Tarnation, so did Paige, but somehow she still couldn't imagine feeling safe herself. Not with him. Not near him.

"You don't consider a teacher low-down, do you?"

"Low-down? Good grief, no."

"Maybe teachers are turkeys in your eyes?"

Obviously something in her expression must have given him a totally wrong impression. "I couldn't possibly think more of teachers, Stefan. They're up there near saint status with me . . . partly because a zillion years ago, I gave so many of them trouble that I'm embarrassed to remember. I was an awful teenager, rebellious and stubborn, real arrogantly sure of myself and blind to other people's feelings—" She shook her head. "Never mind. Just believe me, I couldn't possibly have more respect for teachers."

Stefan leaned back. "You were a rebel? I cannot imagine you ever causing trouble, lambchop."

"Thankfully, it's history. I'm as straight as an arrow now."

"Yes," he murmured. "It is clear to me that being straight like an arrow is important to you. You work at this hard, I think. Did something happen a long time ago?"

Paige wasn't sure how the conversation had so swiftly changed and focused on her. Vaguely she heard his question. More specifically she felt his gaze lasered on her face, studying her as intensely as if he could see shadows in her eyes, see memories.

She could have told him what happened a long time ago. It wasn't as if it were a deep, dark secret. But she was ashamed of it, ashamed of the girl she'd been then, and that wasn't so easy to confess. Not with him.

Candle flames flickered between the two of them. No one else had wandered into the small anteroom in some time. A log fell in the stone hearth, shooting sparks up the chimney. His profile made a clear shadow on the whitewashed walls, a cameo, she thought, of a man as basic as time. A fierce, bearded warrior with hooded brows and brawny shoulders. A man who was dangerous to his enemies, but who would protect his woman and his hearth from all danger.

She mentally shook off the fanciful image, unsure where those silly thoughts were even coming from. The room was just so warm. And in spite of the huge and wonderful dinner, she'd definitely had enough wine. "Are you ready for a little walk in the fresh air?" she asked him.

He had to notice that she'd ignored his question, but he just smiled—and agreed. It took a few minutes to pay the check, and another minute for them to bundle back up in winter coats and scarves.

Outside, it was snowing white teardrops, slow, thick, fat flakes that lingered on the cheeks and stung. They meandered down Main Street, window-shopping at the bakery and Carlson's Book Store and The Emporium. The sidewalks were shoveled clean, so wearing shoes instead of boots was no problem. Even after her toes started to feel numb and her face burn-cold, Paige didn't want to stop walking. The night air was sharp, fresh and invigorating, and the whole walk felt like a time-out with Stefan.

Seeing her town through his eyes was a whole different experience. So typical of him, he inhaled every thing he saw as if he were a thirsty sieve. Walnut Woods was a pretty ordinary Vermont town, with a white-spired church on the hilltop, the green commons in front of the courthouse, homes with yellow lights in the windows. Every morning there was a heated political argument at Simpson's bakery—no one in Vermont was short of independent opinions. But if there was sickness in a family, it was still a neighborhood where friends showed up with a pie or a tuna fish casserole.

Everything was new to Stefan, all the hundred things she took for granted about her town, her life and life-style. Freedom had a different taste when she was with him. He claimed she was opening his world, but Paige thought he was the one opening hers. Certain truths had always been there. She'd just never looked at them. The conflict of loyalties that had so dominated his life had never even touched hers. Choices she took for granted, Stefan had never had.

Eventually they both admitted to being freezing and raced back to the car. Stefan's rental car had a blasting, noisy heater that toasted her toes in no time, and they were still making comfortable, easy conversation the whole drive home. There seemed nothing he wasn't curious about; he asked about neighbors' names, what they did, seemed to take in every story she shared about them. When he pulled into her driveway, she couldn't believe they were already home.

Her house was dark. She'd forgotten to leave on lights. And when she bent her head to fumble in her purse for a house key, she couldn't seem to find that, either.

"Um, lambchop? I would guess that you do not need to worry about the key. I would strongly suspect that your remembering to lock the house, on a scale of one to ten, is about a negative fifty."

She stopped fumbling, and shot him a ferocious glare. "I'd better warn you, Michaelovich, that if you're thinking about teasing me for being absent-minded—"

"No, no. I am a bright man, trust me. I want to live. The sky will snow green before I would suggest that you are even the smallest iota forgetful." But she heard his irrepressible chuckle, just before he climbed out of the car.

She followed him. "Are you laughing at me, Michaelovich?"

"You bet your sweet bippy, lambchop."

Sweet bippy. God, where did he come up with them? "There wasn't a reason on earth why I *needed* to lock the house. There hasn't been a theft around here since I was a kid."

"This is good," he said, still chuckling.

"Just so you know, Stefan—I've leveled bigger men than you for teasing me."

"Ah. Is this a threat?"

"I'm too much of a lady to make threats. It was just a general statement of fact. The sky is blue. The sun comes up in the morning. You risk your life if you tease me."

"Thank you for this helpful statement of fact. Once again, you have me shooking in my boots."

But he didn't seem to be "shooking" when his hand plucked her sleeve. And when she spun around, he was as close as a partner in a dance—a dance in which he was definitely leading. She didn't even have time to correct his grammar about the "shooking" before he suddenly, naturally, easily swung her into his arms.

There wasn't a light on for miles, and it was darker than pitch under the front porch overhang. Even so, she could see his eyes glinting with laughter, and he was smiling when he ducked his head. He kissed her with that smile, his lips still curved, as if he were still teasing her and that kiss was only an extension of his teasing humor.

That illusion lasted a second. Maybe two.

The world was hushed. The snowflakes were soundless; the trees didn't make a single rustle; no cars nor trucks had the courtesy to pass down the road and make nice, noisy crunchy tire sounds. The only thing thundering seemed to be her heart.

Those whiskers of his tickled mercilessly. He smelled like an unbearably cold crisp night, and he tasted like wine and a butterscotch mint, and beneath those flavors, he tasted like *him*. His mouth was smooth and colder than snow...for a second. His lips warmed up fast, connected with hers.

Okay, she thought, okay, as if she were bracing for a shot at the dentist. She'd been through this before and survived just fine. He'd stopped before, and he'd stop again. Pounds and pounds of winter coats were between them. There wasn't a single thing she needed to worry could happen, not outside, not on a ten-degree night on her front porch... and she was hardly going to lose her mind and ask him in.

Shots at the dentist only *seemed* to last forever.

Like this kiss.

Only not quite the same. This kind of kissing definitely hurt, but the hurt was... delicious. Heady. A sting-sharp yearning that started in her toes and moved up through her bloodstream, soft, silent, faster than a surprise and yet slower than she could sigh. It stabbed her heart with a piercing sweetness, but the real source of the hurt, the really unbearable nastiness, was the texture of his mouth.

A hundred years ago, she'd kissed a ton of boys. None that tasted like him. None that felt like him. He was distinctly a virile, physical man, which made for a terrifying and dangerous difference. And he was Stefan, which damn it, made him scarier yet.

Her scarf seemed to have slipped and fallen in the snow. Her arms, propelled by insanity, seemed to have roped around his neck. Her fingers sieved in his thick, unruly hair, feeling it ruffle through her palms as if—more insanity—it was her natural right to touch him.

Somehow a simple kiss turned openmouthed, somehow suddenly involved teeth and tongues. Desire spiraled between them like a drug in the air that neither could escape breathing. Control was important to her. More than important. She didn't lose control, ever, never allowed emotion to trample reason and good sense. Yet wanting him seemed natural, as if she were only sharing a secret that already belonged to Stefan, as if she were safe. She had the craziest, wildest sensation that she could brave rapids, or skydive, or risk any danger on earth and it would be okay with him. Only with him.

Slowly he severed that kiss. Slowly his hands unclenched from her hair and he lifted his head. With the tip of a fingertip he traced the soft cushion of her bottom lip. His eyes, she saw, were no longer smiling, but as grave and dark as that midnight sky. "You must know how I feel, *lyubeesh,*" he murmured. "In your eyes, I see how you feel. And with your kisses, you tell me more."

But she was suddenly fever-dizzy. And her heart was thumping from panic. How could this have happened again? She'd been so sure, if they just spent more time together, that she'd get a handle on those explosive, impulsive sexual feelings. This wasn't *her.* She never behaved this way. "It was just the wine from dinner."

"No." He smoothed back her hair.

"We're *friends.*"

"Yes, I hope this. I feel this." He paused. "And I am well aware that my life is upended right now, much unsettled, no security I can even offer you until I pin down a job. I respect that this is important to a woman, lambchop. But I cannot make you promises quite yet."

Maybe she hadn't recovered from those fevered moments of insanity, because it seemed stark crazy to assume he meant promises along the lines of marriage and rings and commitment. Only Stefan was not like her. He was as emotionally volatile as dynamite, and no more predictable. "Stefan, you're right about being unsettled. You just moved—you're just adopting a new country, and everything is new for you. You have to be lonely and I happened to be here, more than willing to be your friend, but it might be awfully easy to mistake that for something else."

"I understand why you think this. With my background, you have reason to be unsure of my loyalties—"

She shook her head fiercely. "I wasn't talking about loyalties."

Again, he smoothed back the hair from her brow, the hair that he'd tumbled and fisted in his hands in a kiss that was still happening in his eyes. "Oh, yeah, you were," he said quietly. "The loyalty between a man and a woman is powerful and strong and takes immeasurable trust, *lyubeesh*. And I hear that you are not sure. I think I could make you sure . . . so maybe best you go in the house before I invite you into more trouble."

"Stefan—"

"I am not claiming good control right now. I am being honest. I would like to prove to you exactly what is between us—what is, and what could be—and I am very, very tempted by this idea. I think you would like this kind of trouble more than you believe now. I think this trouble would be good for both of us."

"Stefan—"

"Go in house. I tell you now. Last warning. Lock door. Show me you mean no."

Seven

If it hadn't been for a killing problem with thirst, Paige would never have looked up. Since early morning she'd been working with gravers and scorpers and narrow-edged chisels on the coral cameo for Gwen. The project was coming. Splendiferously.

The work required such disciplined concentration that she had no time to think about last night... or a man with eyes so dark, so deep, that a woman could tumble right in and drown. Work was a much, much better thing to focus on than Stefan. And she had, easily paying no attention to her cramping neck muscles or the nag of a lack-of-sleep headache. Her throat, though, was drier than the Sahara at high noon.

Impatiently she glanced around the workshop. Sometime earlier, she *knew* she'd made herself a mug of peppermint tea, but the mug was nowhere in sight.

The darn thing had walked off and gotten itself lost. Again.

Exasperated, she laid down the half-finished cameo on a strip of velvet, and then went on a rescue-search mission for the mug. It wasn't hiding in the bathroom, the hall, the living room. The telephone jangled just as she spotted it on the kitchen windowsill—*now* she remembered, pausing to watch a cardinal in the snow when she'd been making the tea.

It seemed the same forgetful dimwit had forgotten to put on the answering machine, too, because the blasted phone showed no inclination to quit ringing. Gulping several fast sips to soothe her thirst, she hiked for the traveling phone receiver in the hall.

Abby rarely called during the day, but most typically, her oldest sister didn't waste a breath on a hello or how are you. "Couldn't wait to tell you. I'm up for a promotion."

"This is news? You've won a zillion promotions."

"Yeah. But this is the one that matters, the top of everything I've worked for. Two other guys competing for the same slot, but I've outworked and outperformed their records three times over—"

"And you want the job so bad you can taste it?"

In the background of the L.A. office, phones rang and electronic devices clattered and people interrupted—Paige couldn't remember a call from her sister when Abby wasn't trying to do three things at the same time. Still, she heard her sister sigh. "God, you're the only one who understands. Gwen gives me attagirls, but I know she thinks I'm weird. Doesn't seem to matter how many women's lib revolutions we go through. We all think it's okay and natural for a guy to have ambition, but catch a woman trying to climb the corporate ladder, and she's treated like she's flawed or unfeminine or as if something went haywire on her X chromosome. Man, I'm tired of it. I've *earned* this job, Paige. It has *nothing* to do with gender.''

''Hey, you don't have to convince me of anything. I've always been in your cheerleading corner, remember?'' With the phone cradled in her ear, Paige instinctively started pacing.

Technically Abby was relaying good news, but all Paige heard was the exhaustion in her sister's voice. It had been getting worse since Christmas. Abby sounded increasingly stressed to a razor edge, and Paige had long been worried that her oldest sister worked too hard, had somehow confused the difference between a natural ''drive'' and ''being driven''— but it just wasn't easy to get her to talk about it. Such as now, faster than a jet stream, she changed the subject.

''So... how was it? The dinner?''

It was too much to hope that Abby had forgotten, but Paige clipped out a quick answer. ''Awful.''

''Uh-huh. And did he make a pass after dinner?''

''That was awful, too.'' Paige lifted her hand for another sip of tea and discovered the mug had disappeared. Dammit. The darn thing had lost itself *again*.

''Uh-huh. And are you going out with him again?''

''We weren't 'going out' the first time. I probably didn't explain before. Stefan just moved here from Russia, and he happens to have family in Walnut Woods, so it worked for him to rent the old Jasper place until he decides on a job and where he wants to settle. His being here is only a temporary thing, but right now, everything's new for him—he just needs a friend, that's all. To sort of help him get...acclimatized.''

"Hmm. A Russian. How interesting. Sounds exotic and foreign and sexy. Is he cute?''

"Since he's only a *friend,* it wouldn't matter if he were five foot two and homely,'' Paige said irritably.

"I agree with you, but somehow I doubt that he's five foot two and homely. I'm getting a pretty good picture of him, and so far I'm impressed. He'd have to be close to heart-stopping adorable to rattle your cage, Sis, and more to the point, he'd have to be able to outsmart you. It's never been easy for you to find a guy who could outsmart you. He's really bright, huh?''

"Do you have any idea how annoying it can be to talk with you sometimes?''

Abby laughed. "Back to the ranch. He's just 'a friend,' huh? So when he made that pass at you, I take it this was to help him get...acclimatized?''

"No. He only did that because he was confused.''

"Uh-huh. What a fascinating and unusual reason for a guy to kiss a woman.''

"You don't understand. I'm serious. He doesn't even know me, not really. He's just lost right now, finding his way in a whole new place. And he's one of those people with an affectionate, emotional nature. He just tends to express himself...physically. He doesn't necessarily mean anything by it.''

"Paige?''

"*What?*''

"You may be right that he doesn't really know you,'' Abby said gently. "But that's always going to be true, Sis, unless you open the door and *let* him get to know you. And I have to go. Catch you later in the week. But this is an order until we talk again—raise some hell and *don't* be good."

Paige rolled her eyes as she hung up the phone. She reclaimed the missing tea mug from the stair steps, copped a lemon-drop cookie from the kitchen and ambled back to her workshop.

If her sister had control over the red phone in the White House, the country would be in constant war. Abby always voted for action . . . as if action were the only choice. As if letting Stefan getting to know her *was* a choice.

She perched on the work stool, swung a leg around a rung and picked up the coral cameo. Yet she found herself staring at it instead of working. No one, even her sisters, ever understood how she'd ended up in an obscure field such as cameo making. And to anyone who'd known her when she was a teenager, her love for the cameos had to seem especially ironic. Cameos were traditionally a *lady's* choice of jewelry. They were distinctly not brassy like rhinestones, not showy like diamonds or precious gems. A cameo was subtle, tasteful, subdued.

There was a time when she'd been no *lady*.

A time when she'd worn her emotions as out-front and loud as brassy fool's gold.

A time when a boy had died. Maybe because of her. Because she'd behaved the way no lady would behave.

Paige squeezed her eyes closed and swallowed hard. Outsiders had no way to know the chief requirement to carving a good cameo. It wasn't talent, or skill, but a respect for the truth. A sculptor couldn't force the raw material to turn out a certain way, couldn't pretend, couldn't impose what *she* wanted. She had to deal with the truth inherent in that raw material—or risk ruining the piece.

She hadn't been sure last night—and she felt unsure now—what Stefan felt for her. Or what she felt in return. But no matter how annoying her sister could be, Abby could occasionally give out painfully insightful advice. Maybe that was exactly what she had to do to stop this relationship before either of them got hurt . . . let Stefan get to know her. Really know her. And that included all the real truths about the kind of woman she was.

That should nip any feelings he had for her. Right in the bud.

Stefan pulled in her driveway around three in the afternoon with a one-horse open sleigh. Just like in the American song, the harness was studded with a rope of bells. When he reined in under her workshop window, he gave the harness a hearty shake so Paige could hear the jingling bells, and then he waited. Building up his confidence. Building up his courage.

She would not, he suspected, be thrilled to see him. She'd been too shook up when he left her last night. But Paige was predictably absentminded. She just might be coaxed into forgetting her reluctance if he effectively distracted her.

Maybe other men had come knocking; maybe other men had brought roses or scent or chocolates. Stefan couldn't see doing anything that had a possible comparison factor. That tower of hers was more cement than ivory. Whatever those other boys had done, Rapunzel apparently hadn't been coaxed to let down her hair. An element of surprise was definitely required.

His neighbors had helped him come up with this particular, surely foolproof, surprise. A young couple named Bronson raised the Belgians—Willie Nelson was the horse's name; Willie was two years old and trained to pull wagons and sleds, although he had a teensy tendency to run hell-bent for leather. Another neighbor, an old whiskered gentleman named Archibald, had loaned him the antique sleigh and belled harness. Initially the runners on the sleigh had been rusty, but a few hours work and maintenance and the runner blades were now sharp enough to fly.

All he needed was his lady.

Willie Nelson reared his head and pawed the ground impatiently. Stefan felt like doing the same. He jingled the sleigh bells again, then blew on his cold hands. His gaze tracked from window to window, searching for any sign of movement.

Finally he saw a curtain stir. A wedge of light showed in the opening, then disappeared. Seconds later her back door hurled open.

"Stefan! For heaven's sake! It's not like I didn't hear the bells, but I ignored the sound. I figured I was just losing my mind. But when I finally looked out, I realized that it was you who'd lost yours. Where on earth did you get the horse? The sleigh? What—?"

He heard the tornado of questions. He expected the questions, expected the hands on jeaned hips, the floppy socks, the oversize sweatshirt with the droopy neck. But he was braced for reluctance, for serious resistance. Instead he heard the fake bluster in her voice, saw the soft mauve shadows under her eyes and the hectic color in her cheeks. She was unwilling to see him, all right. Unwilling exactly as the night before.

Her brown eyes were huge and aglow, more naked with emotion than she knew.

She was not unwilling. Only skittery. Only scared.

Resolve made his heart hammer with more confidence. It went against every ethical grain to push a woman whose "no" signals had been more than clear. But what Paige said and her actions gave him conflicting messages.

The night before, she'd protected him as if she were a she-lion with every stranger, obviously prepared to defend any language gaff he could make and scooping him into her circle of friends. In her life, she was a loner as he was, someone who shared the need to take a different road. He could tell her anything, and damn near had. She listened. Not just to words. She had the compassion and empathy to listen to a man's heart.

She also kissed... unforgettably. Like a lover claiming her man. Like an explosion of emotion, of sensation, of yearning, so potent that a single kiss from her could go straight to a man's head. Stefan had no idea if she realized how rare and special she was.

He did. And it—almost—struck him as humorous. He'd always been a fighter. He'd fought family, friends, co-workers and country to follow his conscience and the truth of his heart. He'd never feared or backed down from a fight before, yet fighting for her was an entirely different kettle of bees.

He even knew what the difference was.

He had never been scared of losing before.

Rapid-fire, he answered all her how, when and where questions about the horse and sleigh, then cut to the chase. "I was thinking that you might need a break. Is Russian custom in the winter, to take break in the afternoon with a sleigh ride. Fresh air invigorates the soul. Exercise brings new energy. Good idea, yes?''

Actually there was no such custom anywhere in Russia he knew of, but Stefan was adopting his new country's philosophy: A man did what a man had to do. The diversion was working, and for a few minutes, he successfully kept her so spinning-busy moving that she had no time to protest.

It wasn't hard to guess that she hadn't eaten that day, since she never remembered to eat. So he stuffed her with a sandwich first, while he scouted her closet for boots, hat, scarf, jacket and gloves. She needed to be bundled up good—it was a maniacal cold five degrees and starting to snow heavily. And once he had her back outside, trussed up good, he swiftly lifted her into the seat, talking so fast she couldn't possibly get a word in.

"The Belgian's name is Willie Nelson. He is good boy, but must confess, full of hell. Keeping him down will be teensy challenge, I think. Cover with blanket, *lyubeesh,* and there is mulled wine with cinnamon in thermos if you are thirsty—hot, though, take care not to burn mouth—"

"Stefan?"

Well. He had been *trying* to talk so fast that she could not get a word in, but she had managed that one. He vaulted into the seat next to her, and decided since he'd gotten her this far, this close, he could perhaps give her a chance to speak without risking her taking a powder on him. "What?"

"You've called me *'lyubeesh'* several times, but I don't know what it means."

He'd brought a blanket to seal out the cold, and now he carefully tucked it around her legs—and his. Their eyes only met for the flash-of-a-flame second. "*Lyubeesh* just means lover," he said simply.

He intended to flick the reins and take off—Willie Nelson was hot to trot, and Stefan figured speed was a real, real good idea about then. But she laid a gloved hand on his arm. And beneath that hectic color on her cheeks, her skin was suddenly as pale as paper.

"I was afraid it meant something like that," she said slowly, "and I think we'd better talk. I need to tell you something, Stefan, and I need you to listen."

Out this story spilled, so fast that Stefan had trouble following. It seemed that when the three Stanford sisters were growing up, Abby and Gwen had been as good as gold. Not Paige. She claimed she drove her parents nuts worrying about her. She'd been a rebel, a troublemaker, a daredevil.

In high school, she'd worn short skirts and tight sweaters and enough makeup to financially support the mascara industry. Stefan was unsure of the mascara word, but he picked up the drift. She was ashamed of this girl she had been. And it shamed her to tell him this story—yet she persisted. There'd been no end to the trouble she volunteered for. She flirted with all the boys, stayed out late, skipped school, guzzled beer, indulged in crazy pranks. She was Ms. Cool. The leader of the wild pack. And the boys lined up to go out with her.

"There was a reason for my so-called popularity," she admitted painfully. "I knew exactly what the boys thought. They were real sure I was the kind of girl who'd put out—"

"Put out?"

Her eyes dropped, and seemed to fixate on his shoulder. "Put out means to sleep with, to have sex with. The boys assumed because I was the wildest girl in school that I must be easy. And I didn't do anything to correct that reputation, even though it wasn't true. The point was...I liked the attention. I liked the boys chasing me. I loved that whole kick of hormones, loved that I could attract them."

When she ran out of breath for a second, Stefan unscrewed the thermos and poured her a cupful of wine. She drained the whole cup in big gulps, but the wine neither seemed to calm nor slow her down. She went on.

"There was a boy named Johnny, who trailed after me as faithfully as a hound. He just wasn't cool enough for me to go out with, Stefan—and if that sounds insensitive and cruel, all I can tell you is that that's how I was then. So Johnny decided to do something real wild to catch my attention. One Saturday night, around two in the morning, he slugged down a six-pack and gunned his dad's Chevy going down Main Street. Only he wrapped himself around a lamppost. And he died."

Stefan's heart slowed way down. He couldn't stop looking at her face. Snowflakes landed on her cheeks, her chin, and her eyes were glistening from the cold, but beneath that, her skin looked so pale. And her expression, so fragile. It cost her to confess this whole traumatic tale, and from the look in her eyes, she seemed positive that this story would completely change his opinion of her.

It *did* change things, but not, perhaps, the way she intended. All along, he'd sensed she was afraid of something. But all along, he'd thought it was something about him that worried her, not that she had some burden chewing like a raw sore on her soul. "And you have blamed yourself for this, lambchop?" he asked quietly.

"I didn't make him drink the beer. I didn't make him race the car. And believe me, I had no idea what he intended to do. But yeah . . . I blamed myself."

She met his eyes with painful honesty. "I let hormones rule my whole life when I was teenager. Maybe the accident would never have happened if I hadn't been so insensitive, so blind to that boy's feelings. And I turned myself around from that girl I used to be, Stefan. I wanted to do that, needed to do that, but the thing is . . . I really *did* change. I'd make a terrible *'lyubeesh'* for you. Trust me. There's a good chance I'd bore a lover to death. I'm a dead-serious lady these days. Discipline and control are really important to me—"

"Important to you to be straight-arrow now," he interjected, remembering when she had brought up that phrase before.

"Yes. It is."

"Love is . . . messy. You let leopard out of bag, and who knows? Could be chaos. Could be out of control. Could be hurt. I know chaos theory well. Mathematical nightmare."

"You understand," she said. He could hardly miss her huge exhaled sigh of relief.

"Am very glad you explained. Understand many, many things much better now." No snowflake landed on her cheek at that instant, but he pretended one did. It gave him the excuse to brush the pad of his thumb across her soft, soft skin. "But we would not throw the whole world into chaos, I think, by going on a

sleigh ride. Have fun, laugh together, few minutes
sleigh ride... these are little things. No risking any of
that nasty chaos that I can see."

She chuckled, a little nervously, but her smile was
real. "You're right. Let's go for it," she said lightly.

He instantly clicked the reins. As if Willie Nelson
had only been waiting for permission, the frisky Belgian took off. Perhaps Stefan had sharpened the runner blades a little too well, because they skimmed the
glazed snow surface at luge speeds.

Her yard disappeared from sight, then his, and that
was the last of the view of civilized buildings. Snow
pelted down. The bells jangled faster than rock 'n'
roll. Wind burned their cheeks like fire. They headed
for an open meadow, where the whole snowy landscape looked diamond-dipped and blinding bright.
Beneath the snow, though, no matter how thick the
layers, Vermont seemed to hide a lot of stones. The
sleigh teetered once. Then again.

Stefan figured he'd better take charge and slow
down Willie Nelson before the sleigh overturned and
tossed them both... but then Paige laughed.

Really laughed. As he'd never heard her laugh before. Maybe she'd been in no mood for laughter minutes before, but the peel of a throaty female chuckle
escaped from her. That chuckle helplessly escalated
into a carefree, outright, can't-help-it-if-I-feel-joyful
belly laugh. She was *happy*... and loving this ride.

To hell with whether the sleigh overturned. Stefan
gave Willie Nelson free rein. They flew over the field
on dancing wings, racing, chasing, the snow coming
down in bushels now and blanketing their hats and
shoulders with white. A stand of pines with a silver-
running creek loomed ahead. Willie needed a rest,

whether he realized it or not, and when Stefan finally pulled up the reins, both animals and humans were exhilarated and breathless.

He let out a roar of exuberant laughter for the sheer joy of it. And so did she.

"That was insane and crazy," she said.

"Insane and crazy... and good fun."

"*Great* fun," She corrected him with another grin. She looked at him, her eyes full of light and laughter, snowflakes melting in her hair, her face so damn beautiful he just wanted to look at it. And look some more. Too soon, though, way too soon, her smile faded. "Stefan—"

She was worrying about chaos again, he suspected. She was worrying about a boy named Johnny from a long time ago. And he felt unsure exactly what that whole convoluted story meant to her, but he was pretty sure about some of the highlights. Somehow his lady had convinced herself that some terrible, reprehensible hell would break loose if she dared let go of her emotions.

He pushed her hat off, framed her face between his gloved hands and kissed her. The kiss was not meant to reassure her. He could not. What she feared was a probable risk. All hell broke loose when he kissed her. And the chaos loomed as a guaranteed threat whenever she kissed him back.

Their lips met, clung, heated. Bodies warmed to tropical temperatures. Willie Nelson, perhaps suddenly realizing the damn fool Russian had finally dropped his guard, tried a couple of dance steps forward, and when no one yanked his reins, took off at at a fox-trot.

Stefan didn't give a damn. It seemed all he could give her was exactly what she was afraid of. Risk. Of the most monumental kind. But her self-perception, this perceived need of hers to be a button-down straight arrow, was both wrong and crippling to the woman he had come to know. His lover was so painfully full of emotion. So exquisitely full of passion. So beautiful—so giving, so caring and sensitive, and so full of love. She tasted like mulled wine and snowflakes. She tasted like desire. She tasted like a woman who could drive him straight to the cliff of chaos—and tip him off for the sheer feminine pleasure of it.

The sleigh teetered. His hand groped blindly for the reins. She had her arms around his neck at that moment, and he wasn't about to sever a kiss just because their lives were in imminent peril. When Paige was feeling high and heady and wild on her feminine powers, life and death issues seemed pretty paltry.

"Whoa," Paige whispered.

Willie Nelson, as if expecting the humans to finally come to their senses, slowed up.

"Whoa," Paige said again.

The Belgian tossed his head on the snort of a sigh, gave in and stopped.

She wasn't talking to the horse. Her eyes were on his. Luminous, dark, dazed eyes, with the truth reflected in them like a mirror. It was herself she was trying to "whoa." Not him.

He was not the enemy she feared. Stefan would have willingly slayed dragons for her, but he had no idea how to slay a dragon that was locked, padlocked-tight, in her own heart.

Eight

No saint could feel more self-righteous. When Paige pulled into her driveway, she'd leveled her entire rotten chore list—gas, groceries, drugstore; she'd express-mailed an order of cameos to Harry and hit the bank. She'd even fed the bank some money before she was overdrawn.

Carrying packages, she hustled inside and peeled off her jacket, ignoring the bills on the counter—she'd been virtuous for about as long as she could stand—and aimed straight for the refrigerator. She'd missed lunch, and her stomach was growling like a restless bear. She had in mind a peanut butter and jelly sandwich.

As quickly as she opened the refrigerator door, she saw the Raspberry Fool concoction on the first shelf. Stefan had brought it over on Monday, told her it was made with raspberries, sugar, cream and a splash of rum. There was—maybe—two bites of it left.

On the second shelf was the gift he'd carted over on Tuesday. With the devil's own grin, he claimed the recipe was called Cream and Sugar Slave, and the ingredients in *that* temptation were vanilla, sour cream, dark brown sugar and real cream, all heaped on top with a mound of fresh blueberries. There was—maybe—two slices of that one left.

Yesterday he'd brought over the White Chocolate Passion Fruit Mousse. She didn't know what all was in it. She didn't want to know. It was beyond decadence. It could drive a nun to sin. And no, she hadn't been able to resist that, either.

Paige slammed the refrigerator door closed, no longer in any mood for peanut butter. No longer in any mood for anything.

The man was a menace to her health.

She glanced at the kitchen clock. It was just past one. Plenty of time to get a couple of hours work in before the Russian Menace popped over for *Star Trek*—and did something new and dangerous to destroy her life *that* day.

She hustled upstairs to change into working clothes, thinking that she needed to do something about that man. Something soon. Something effective.

The trick was knowing *what*.

In her bedroom, she peeled off her town jeans and dived into a skinny sweater and overalls. She was just reaching for socks when her elbow bumped a heap of things on the dresser. A linen pillowcase slipped to the carpet, revealing the jade cameo. She'd almost forgotten covering the cameo in a fit of aggravation, but she easily remembered why she'd done it now. The jade woman glowed in the pale afternoon light, invoking the same uneasy, disturbing feelings she had from the start.

It was past time she dealt with that problem.

Impatiently, determinedly, Paige turned the cameo woman to face the dresser mirror, then hunched over the mirror herself and studied both. Heaven knew why she hadn't done it before. The comparison factor was immediately and enormously reassuring. She was nothing like that wanton, sensual woods nymph. Her braid was comfortingly, familiarly skewed, with messy tendrils escaping all over the place; her face was clean, no show-off makeup; and her clothes were practical old friends. She looked exactly what she was. A worker. A serious person. A plain old sturdy, responsible woman...leaning toward the dull, ordinary side.

And dammit, she'd *told* Stefan. Told him that whole shaming story about Johnny, just so he would know that she had done things she was ashamed of, things that should have made him doubt her character. God knows, she did. And she'd been honest with him about being pit-rotten lover material.

She just wasn't the type, not anymore, to entice a guy or blithely throw caution to the wind. It wasn't sex that was the problem. Or having an affair, or falling in love. It was just that there had to be rules. She had to be in control. That was one of the rules. It had taken her years—long years—to build up a mountain of repressive inhibitions, and she was well aware that most men hardly appreciated those ingredients in a lover. Somewhere out there, she kept thinking that there had to be some men who were handily, happily repressed, too.

Stefan wasn't one of them.

Stefan probably couldn't define "inhibition" with a Russian dictionary, if his life depended on it.

Paige slugged her hands into her overall pockets and hiked downstairs toward her workroom. Every embrace they'd shared clung in her mind in technicolor; every word replayed in stereo. All those memories shook her up. But he'd kissed her on that crazy sleigh ride as if he never noticed she was shook up. He'd kissed her as if she were the only woman on his planet, and then he came bearing presents. And more presents. He was more underfoot than a new puppy.

Stefan was lonely. And he was going to move on. It was only for a temporary period that he needed someone, and she was handy. Any minute now, he'd come to his senses and realize how impossibly different they were. She'd been straight and honest and completely herself with him. For that matter, he had made no pass since that winsome, wild afternoon on the sleigh, so maybe he *had* come to his senses.

Maybe he was just trying to tempt her beyond all sanity with desserts.

She closed the door on her workshop, switched on lights, opened her tool drawers and took out Gwen's coral. The cameo was coming fast now, but even the slightest mistake at this point could ruin the whole piece. Forget him and concentrate, she told herself.

And she did. For a while. But some instinct made her glance at the clock when it was four. It was time for *Star Trek* to start, and he wasn't here. There was a break, she told herself.

Except that he hadn't shown up by four-thirty, either. Certainly there was no reason he *had* to show up for *Star Trek*—or for that matter, at all—but it was the first day he hadn't. Her relief was enormous, and a measure of how much dread-anticipation she'd been living on, never sure when he was going to show, what he was going to do. For the first afternoon in weeks, she could *really* work in peace.

But his absence started to itch on her nerves. He *always* showed up. What if he were sick? What if he'd fallen down the basement stairs in the old Jasper house and broken a leg and no one knew? What if he'd taken a chain saw to some firewood and hurt himself and was lying bleeding somewhere? Who was there to check on him?

If she didn't?

She decided to give him until six o'clock to bug her.

But at six o'clock, he hadn't bugged her. Hadn't called. Hadn't sneaked anything new and disgracefully decadent into her refrigerator. And she found herself standing at the front windows in the living room, hands on her hips, trying to peer over the stone fence and past the pines to see if there were lights on in his house.

Unfortunately she couldn't see his car or his lights or anything else—not from any window view in her house. There was no way to know anything for sure unless she hiked outside to look.

She grabbed her down jacket, thinking all she was going to do was make sure he was alive. That was it. No visit. No big deal. She was just going to say, hi, how are you, just wanted to make sure you weren't dead, and when he answered in the affirmative, she'd leave right away.

There seemed something flawed in the plan, but the alternative was pacing around and worrying about him all evening. Better to go. She jogged across the road, memorizing her escape lines, noticing his car as she aimed for the front door, noticing no lights. The outside clues weren't providing enough evidence to help her draw any conclusions without going in.

She rapped on the back storm door. Then rapped again. No answer. She poked her head in, yoohooing, "Stefan?"

No answer to that, either.

Her pulse started scrabbling erratically. Even if the man were a menace to her health, even if he'd badly disturbed her from the day she met him...she'd die if he was hurt. It was one thing to lose car keys and forget to eat and sort of misremember to balance her checking account. She was used to losing things, but the fear of losing Stefan was an entirely different dimension. She never anticipated such panic that something could have happened to him. Somewhere, somehow, he had come to matter to her. Deeply, painfully matter.

She hadn't been in the house since old man Jasper lived here—who'd terrorized all three sisters growing up, undoubtedly because they'd stolen raspberries from his backyard. The house layout was familiar enough to get around, though. A barn-size red kitchen led to a gloomy dark hall. She peeked into the laundry utility room, then a bathroom with an old-fashioned claw-foot tub.

She wasn't going into the bedroom wing, she decided, because it would be impossibly awkward if she found him dressing or napping. Unless she hadn't found him before then, in which case she'd just have to awkward-it out.

Her shoulders still hunched in her jacket—uncontestable proof she had no intention of staying—she rounded a corner into the living room. In old man

Jasper's time, the walls had been painted the color and
texture of cottage cheese; the room was stuffed with
oversize furniture and the chief decoration had been
a polished gun rack.

The guns were gone, the walls now painted a muted
French blue. Wood was neatly stacked on the fieldstone hearth, a snap-and-crackle fire lapping the logs
in the grate. The ponderous furniture had been re-
placed with a thick-cushioned navy couch and a
mountain of high-tech equipment. She noted the TV
and stereo, but her gaze instantly zoomed on the maze
of a complex computer setup that had to challenge the
electric system in the house.

Stefan was there. In front of the monitor. Dressed
comfortably in a buffalo plaid shirt, jeans, and bare
feet—huge bare feet. Her first inclination was to
thwack him a good one upside the head. For Pete's
sake, she'd yoohooed his name a dozen times and
worried herself to a near tizzy, and he'd not only ignored her but looked happier and healthier than a
contented clam.

She never delivered that whomp, though. Even at
first glance, she could see how hard he was concentrating. His eyes were intensely focused, his brow fur-
rowed. Papers were stashed next to him higher than
the windowsill. A zillion numbers showed on the
monitor, and he was still keyboarding in more. His
thick hair was rumpled, as if he'd shoveled a hand
through it countless times.

Just like her. The thought lodged in her mind as if
it were a sudden sliver. Over and over she'd told herself that Stefan was as unlike her as a fussbudget
beaver and a wild, uncivilized bear. He was nothing
like the nice, safe, repressed intellectual type she'd al-

ways enjoyed fantasizing about . . . but in this, she'd just never expected to find a kindred spirit. Her damn Russian looked just like her when she was working, totally immersed, oblivious to fires or tornadoes or anything else . . . not even hearing someone yelling his name from the next room. And no one, but no one, could understand that love of work or intense concentration as well as she could.

Paige pivoted around, thinking she'd just tiptoe out of here—he hadn't noticed her yet—since she now knew for sure that he was okay. Yet she hesitated.

She'd bet a blue-chip stock that he hadn't eaten. She'd even bet her favorite pair of Uggs that he'd forgotten all about food. And guilt roiled within her conscience. Maybe she hadn't asked, maybe she hadn't wanted him to, but Stefan had been doing a dozen favors and chores for her. He'd given and given and given. And although he'd stolen a few kisses—and cracked a fissure on her sanity in the process—he had never asked for, nor even seemed to expect anything in return for all those nice things he'd done.

Slowly she peeled off her jacket, and winged it on a chair. Slowly she came up behind him and put a hand on his shoulder. "Stefan, it's just me." She expected him to half jump out of his skin—and probably bark her head off. It was what she'd have done if somebody had suddenly interrupted her concentration.

Yet his left hand immediately reached up and covered hers, as if he weren't startled by her presence at all. He said, "I'm glad you're here, lambchop. But I cannot stop what I am doing at exactly this second."

And he didn't stop—the fingers on his right hand kept poking keys, making more strange numbers and symbols show up on the monitor. But his left hand seemed to weigh on hers as if it were a lead cuff, holding her hand tightly, warmly to his shoulder.

She managed to twist her hand free, but then she had to roll her eyes. What irony. It was extremely clear that Stefan was going to put work before a woman. Any sane woman was supposed to be smart enough to steer clear of a guy whose priorities were not on her. But damnation, she understood. There were times she got immersed, too, and just never figured any guy would understand that it wasn't a matter of not caring, but that certain types of work were really sabotaged if you were interrupted in the concentration process.

She said, "I'm going to make you some dinner."

No response.

"Stefan. I'm going to make you some dinner, and I don't know what there is in the kitchen, but it's bound to take me at least a half hour to throw something together. You have some time, but you need to start gearing down. You're quitting to eat something, and that's that. If you want to go back to work after dinner, I won't bug you."

No response.

"Say yes so I know this is registering at some brain level," she ordered him firmly.

"Yes, you beautiful, adorable, understanding and irresistible woman."

A simple yes would have done, but she told herself it was unfair to hold any verbal comments he made against him just then. Hells bells, she tended to babble when she was working hard, too.

In the kitchen, she scouted drawers and cupboards for potential dinner ingredients. Unlike her house, he had a full larder of choices. Stefan was a hedonist in more areas than one. Her cooking skills couldn't match him, either—he wasn't getting any Russian Creams or Cream and Sugar Slave concoctions out of her. Regretfully he didn't have any Lean Cuisine. Microwave button-pressing was really her best cooking specialty.

But she couldn't mess up pasta too badly. And he had some fancy gourmet spaghetti-sauce stuff, and plenty of fixings for a fresh salad. She saw an unopened bottle of red wine, but guessed he'd rather have coffee in case he wanted to work later. She made the coffee, fussed with a salad dressing and found the ingredients for fresh rolls.

Fifteen minutes before it was done, she called from the doorway, "Stefan, fifteen-minute warning." And when she got no answer, ordered him, "Say yes so I know there's a functioning connection."

"Yes, love."

No matter how fast he was mastering the language, there was just no curing him of using endearments with her. She'd just accepted that a leopard couldn't change all its spots. Yet that "love" still made her pause, made her pulse suddenly beat like the flutter of butterfly wings. He was getting no more warnings about dinner, she thought darkly. As it happened, he didn't need any. Just as she finished setting silverware on the bar countertop, she spun around to find Stefan in the doorway.

He moved right in to help, took a fork to test the bubbling pasta and then tossed the salad. She didn't know any men who felt comfortable in a kitchen, yet they worked like a natural team together. For a few minutes. By accident their hips bumped when she was moving dishes to the counter, and that comradely team feeling was suddenly all done. There was no smell of sulfur, but there might as well have been a charge of lightning between them. She was suddenly aware of his hip, his body, his hands, his eyes. And he kept sliding glances her way that ignited more lightning charges. What happened to the nice, safe, distracted man who'd been buried in an intellectual physics problem only minutes before?

"You saved my life," he told her. "I would have forgotten all about dinner."

"Happens to me all the time. I understand. You probably want to work again this evening—"

"No need. I'm done. I solved the megillah I was dealing with."

Her eyebrows arched. "Megillah?"

"Did I use the wrong word again?"

"I don't know. I've never heard that one before."

"So even an American has a tough time keeping up with slang," he teased her. "Megillah is like... brouhaha. Big deal. A problem to make a man crazy until it is solved."

She waved her hand in between bites of spaghetti. "I have to warn you not to explain any further. I don't know zip about physics."

"I don't know zip about cameos. But I think we both love our work exactly the same way, yes?" He'd leveled the spaghetti and salad, and now pushed the plates aside. "I knew too many people whose job meant nothing more than making a living. I always felt lucky this way, to find a career and work that was really important to me. I am sorry I ignored you when you first came in, toots."

"It was okay. Really okay."

"Well, I do dishes now while you put feet up. No, don't argue. This division of labor is only fair when you did the cooking. But I would appreciate your watching Dan Rather with me. He requires much translation."

Paige had planned to leave. She'd never, in fact, planned to stay long enough to share the meal with him. When she'd walked over, the skies had already been darkening, but now it was seriously blacker than pitch outside. Time for good girls to be home, and she'd been a card-carrying good girl for more than ten years now.

"The evening news," he said helplessly, "really confuses me. Someone comes on, and announces the facts about some big important issue. Then someone else comes on, and contradicts all the facts that the first person swore to. I don't get it. How you know who is telling the truth. How you know who to believe. This is another cultural gap problem I have been having. It would really help if you would watch with me. Perhaps you could explain so I could understand better."

Well, spit, she thought glumly. She could well believe he was having trouble understanding American politics—especially as interpreted by the news. But somehow, even the simplest questions with Stefan, had a way of sidetracking into the complex. Some minor items on the news miraculously turned into a discussion on the nature of the American press and its relationship to the constitutional right of free speech.

After that, he wanted to know about race relations, and consumerism, and Americans' feelings about religion and the educational system, and the reason for crime and high school dropouts.

The news had been over for two hours before she realized how long she'd been installed on his couch. It wasn't the first time Stefan had conned her into these discussions. He had an insatiable hunger and love of talking about anything American, and she had long suspicioned that he was a ton better read in American history than she was. He just loved this stuff.

At some point, he'd poured her a glass of wine, fed the fire and switched off the TV. His couch was one of those dangerous ones, where you sat down and the cushions swallowed you and the odds were iffy you could ever get up again. And she'd curled up because, after all, she'd been up and working since five that morning, and curling up in her stocking feet was a perfectly reasonable thing to do.

But curling up next to him was not so reasonable.

"...I think there is no inner city in the world where despair is not a problem," he was saying. "It was no different in Russia. Alcoholism and suicide rates very high..."

He'd naturally thrown his arm across the couch back. And it seemed that she had naturally leaned against his arm when she'd gotten animated and distracted by the discussion. She just couldn't remember the exact moment when his hand had dropped, in a way that brushed her shoulder and neck, and his fingers seemed to be sifting a strand of her hair, in a whisper-light, whisper-soft rhythmic caress. The warmth in his eyes was familiar...too familiar.

The fire crackled and hissed, shooting sparks up the chimney. The lemon-orange flames were the only light in the room...and it wasn't enough light. On a blizzard-raw night, the warmth and shadows created a cocoon, a feeling of intimacy, and so did that look in his eyes. She was used to it, she told herself. He always aroused an instinct of danger, of uncomfortable vulnerability, and nothing had happened before. Nothing was different tonight. There was no specific reason to feel that she was suddenly sitting on a warm, gentle, euphoric time bomb.

"... Drugs like crack are in Russian cities, too. But the reason for despair is so much clearer there. The free time of young people is rigidly controlled. They are ever expected to conform, to obey, choices made for them that they have no say in. Poverty is always a cage, but there are so many more choices here. So much hope to just ... Paige?"

"Hmm?"

"Somehow I don't think your mind is still on the despair of the young people who drop out of your high schools?"

"Oh, it is," she assured him.

"Yes? And do you also agree with my assessment about elephants flying?"

"I couldn't agree more," she assured him.

He smiled at her then. A slow, satisfied, distinctly male smile that seemed to come from nowhere. "It was kind of you to come over tonight. You were worried that I was all right, yes?"

"You missed *Star Trek.* I thought you might have been hurt or sick—"

"You care," he announced.

The deep, dark, intimate look in his eyes was sending alarm bells peeling through her pulse. "You're a friend. Of course I care."

"I think, *lyubeesh,* that you like that word 'friend' very much. But it's time to let it go."

"I don't know what you mean—"

"It means I hope you left nothing burning at your house, because I doubt that you're going home tonight. And I don't believe either of us are going to notice any fires. Except for the ones we start here."

"Stefan..." As automatically as the sun came up in the morning, her lips framed a denial. She meant to say no. It never occurred to her that she wouldn't. When he reached for her, she understood what was happening. She understood what she was inviting. There was no possible way to misunderstand the burn-clear desire to seduce her that shone in his eyes.

"Beam me up, Paige Stanford," he murmured, his voice as rough and low as a whisper of wind. Or a dare. And then he kissed her.

He'd kissed her before. Tons of times now. She knew his taste, knew the texture of his mouth, knew the terrorizingly dizzy thing his kisses did to trample her common sense and sanity. She knew how to protect herself from risks that were simply too dangerous. But nothing was the same this night.

His arms swallowed her in a lonely, hungry embrace. She didn't know that he'd been leashing that hunger, didn't know all those other kisses had been his version of polite. When his mouth took hers this time, there was no "please" or "may I" implied. This kiss was a demand. Fierce. Hard. Consuming. He wasn't asking for her response. He was claiming it, and a thrill shot through her like a jagged spear of lightning. So did fear.

She was in love with him. Not a little, but so deeply and painfully that nothing else seemed to matter. She knew he was leaving soon. She believed that loneliness propelled his feelings for her rather than anything that could last. She could list a hundred practical, serious reasons why making love with him was a terrible idea, but Paige had always revered truth, had always been ruthless with herself about facing it. Stefan had long captured a corner of her heart. There wasn't a man on the planet who ever tempted or exasperated or stirred her the way he did. He was beyond special to her. She could no longer deny it.

Maybe her heart already knew that making love with him was inevitable. But she'd counted on him being polite. She'd counted on those other kinds of kisses—the familiar ones. She expected fire, but she had no possible life experience to prepare her for handling a conflagration...

He scooped her into his arms, lifting her from the couch as if she weighed nothing—when she was a solid, sturdy one hundred thirty pounds and utterly embarrassed by such a hokey romantic gesture. She was no princess to be carried off. She was no pirate's booty to be swept away. Yet he kissed her and kept kissing her, into the shadows beyond the firelight, down the gloomy dark hall, his tongue diving into her mouth, inviting fierce, frightening feelings that she wasn't remotely prepared for.

"Stefan, you're scaring me."

"Good," he said.

"We need . . . I need . . . to go slower."

"Nyet. I don't think so. Slow for me—good idea. Slow for you—worst idea in town. And this first time is definitely for you."

He was not giving her sane, rational answers. Never mind if her arms were looped around his neck. Never mind if she allowed him to dip down for another kiss. He wasn't even *trying* to reassure her. And the way her heart was slamming, her heart already knew that he was everything she was afraid of. "We can't make love. I don't have any birth control."

"Lucky thing that I am grown man. No man of honor would ever risk a woman." He kissed her throat, right where her tattletale pulse was racing a hundred miles an hour of sheer feminine nerves. "Only irresponsible boy would not be prepared."

"Stefan—"

"I am right here. Going nowhere. Trust me. You can take that promise for gold."

She squeezed her eyes closed. He was distracting her, and somehow she needed to get some critical information said. "Stefan . . . maybe I haven't done this a million times before."

"I guessed you haven't done it at all," he murmured, his tone as blunt and rough as a burr. "But I am in love with you, *lyubeesh*. Head over knees in love. Beyond reason in love. And this is the way it should be, that you make love only with someone who loves you. And I hear all your stalling questions. I hear the fears in your voice. But unless I have missed something completely in this conversation—I am not hearing a no."

A no wasn't precisely on her mind. An unnamed panic was. Backing out struck her as a superb idea, the best idea she'd had in weeks, maybe the best idea she'd had in her whole life. But then he dropped her on the bed, and followed, coming down on her, with her. Only the palest light glowed from the hall. The double bed had some kind of feather mattress, old-fashioned and swallowing soft. Over that was a spread in some slippery fabric that felt icy, shivery cool beneath her neck.

He wasn't. His body temperature could melt any iceberg. He threw the pillows onto the floor and her head went flat, sinking into the mattress, propelled by a kiss that stole her breath. His fingers snapped the band holding her braid. He lifted his head from that kiss, allowing her to haul in a lungful of air, yet in the same moment her sweatshirt was sweeping over her head. On the sweatshirt's way hurled across the room, her hair came loose. Tumbling loose. Wild loose. Encouraged by his hands tangled in it.

He wasn't giving her time to think. She frantically needed that time. She'd had a cage of inhibitions padlocked for years. That lock was supposed to be made of steel. But damn him, she hadn't been this shook up since she was a girl.

"You're going to be disappointed," she whispered, warning him fiercely, clearly. Honestly.

"I don't think there's a prayer of your doing that, lambchop." Eyes blacker than the devil's suddenly danced . . . as he scooched off her overalls, unraveling her underpants at the same time. "Try, though. In fact, I think is exquisite idea. I think you should try very hard to disappoint me, love. Give it best shot."

His tongue laved the arch of her foot—an insane place to kiss a woman. His tongue, his mouth, traced the curve of her calf. Then her knee. Then the inside of her thigh. She swallowed, then swallowed again, then gave up trying to breathe. "We talked about chaos. I thought you understood—"

"I do understand. Insane thing, to invite chaos. Very frightening, to lose control, to not know what could happen, to upset whole orange cart." He smiled. As he unhooked the front catch of her bra. "This kind of chaos is the most delicious thing in universe that I know. This kind of chaos is terrible risk, no guarantees, nothing for sure. And make no mistake, *lyubeesh*. I am asking you to take this risk with me. I am daring you."

Dare. Stefan couldn't know how that word echoed painfully from her teenage years. Back then, she never turned down a dare, never realized there were consequences for taking blind, impulsive risks that could hurt other people. Paige had buried that woman-child who had caused so much harm. Completely buried. There were simply risks she never took. Not anymore.

At that instant, though, she was bare and he was still fully clothed. And until that instant, everything had happened so fast, so swept-away fast, that she couldn't think, never had a chance to think, didn't have to think. Only suddenly Stefan stopped.

He was lying right next to her. Only inches away. As if a slow motion camera, his dark gaze took in her naked body from toes to tummy to throat, making her feel unbearably exposed and vulnerable. Yet he didn't touch her, made no move to continue that mind-dizzying erotic seduction. When his eyes shot back to hers, they held the black flame of desire, the raw honesty of need. Desire for *her*, need for *her*. Long, silent seconds ticked by, and yet still he did nothing, just waited, waited, waited.

With a groan of frustration she lunged for him. It wasn't livable, feeling exposed to him this way, feeling *dared* by those smoky dark eyes. She pushed at the buttons on his buffalo plaid shirt. Pushed at the snap on his jeans, pushed at the zipper, pushed at the denim fabric.

Maybe it was only for this moment, this night, this lonely stretch in his life that he needed her. And she wanted to be that woman he needed, but she knew her movements were more awkward than seductive. It wasn't something she could help. He was stuck with an unskilled, shook-up lover. She was no good at this. She'd been afraid too long of letting go to ever be good at this.

Stefan didn't seem to get it. He responded as if every awkward, frantic movement she made was worth gold, as if she was worth priceless, treasured gold. He rewarded every damn thing she did with more wooing kisses, more ruthlessly intimate caresses, his pace matching her own wildness and encouraging, coaxing more.

Shadows spun. Somehow the spread slithered to the floor. Somehow blankets bunched beneath them. Somehow she forgot about being awkward and tense and turned hot, fever hot, for him, only for him. It was entirely his fault. Stefan was an earthy, lusty, hopeless hedonist who seemed utterly incapable of even noticing her inhibitions. He savored every plane and hollow of her body, with no mercy and more of that ruthless tenderness, and damn him, seemed to expect her to do the same.

His chest hair was the same dark coal as his beard, woolly, thick, as exotic to explore as his long rangy limbs. His textures, his scent, the hoarse sounds he made of praise and approval, that wicked tongue of his...she couldn't get enough, could never have anticipated that learning him this way would be exciting and terrifying and so completely consuming.

Swearing in Russian, he suddenly reared back and pawed through the pile of clothes in the darkness for a condom. He was back and sweeping her beneath him before her mind even registered what he was doing. He seemed to have forgotten all his English. He kept whispering to her in Russian, a slew of rough-soft, gruff-tender murmurs that he seemed to expect her to understand. She did. She could hardly miss the message in those wet-ebony black eyes. He was daring her again. Making fierce, intimate, unreasonable dares. In his eyes was the demand that she trust him. In his eyes was the desire to unravel every last ounce of sanity she had.

And the whole time he was talking to her, she felt the hot, smooth, shaft-hardness of his arousal, pressing, nudging, daring the entrance to the most vulnerable part of her. She expected to regain some sanity then, because she anticipated pain. How could it not hurt this first time?

And it did hurt, but she never anticipated a hurt this wondrous, this so beyond anything she knew. He moved so slowly, filling that emptiness, and it was as if her body knew him, intimately stretching to accommodate him, to take him in, to make him part of her. She felt as if she belonged, not to him, but with him, and his face was taut and strong and clear even in the shadows.

"*Ya tebya lyublu,*" he whispered. "I love you. Love you, Paige." Then a sudden smile after those grave words, a spare smile, dark with frustration and control and sheer wicked pleasure. "And you'd better hold on, lambchop. Because we're about to take that trip straight to chaos."

She couldn't answer, couldn't respond. Not when need suddenly clawed her by the throat. He started moving, thrusting inside her, catching the pulse and pace of rhythm almost like music, a slow dance spinning into a symphony crescendo. His skin dampened, slickened, glowed. So did hers. Desire burned, hotter than friction, spurring emotions that she swore she couldn't feel, didn't know she could feel, spurring a rage of need for release.

This chaos was everything she'd been afraid of.

And more precious than anything she'd ever dreamed of.

It was him, she thought in those last few seconds before release finally exploded within, without, all through her. This could never have been right with anyone else. Could never have happened with anyone else. Only Stefan.

That thought, that emotion, comet-tailed her spin into ecstasy.

It was only later that she remembered there were huge and unignorable prices to pay for losing control. And the piper was waiting with the bill.

Nine

Sometime in the wee hours, Stefan wakened to the sounds of a snowstorm. The wind lashed and wailed, thwacking branches against the windows and hurling hard-driving bullets of snow. It was an ideal night to burrow down, hibernating deep under the covers, preferably cuddled with a lover.

Stefan even had the lover he wanted to hibernate with, but sometime during the night Paige had escaped his cuddle. She wasn't far. Only a pillow away. It appeared that she'd been studiously chewing on a fingernail and staring blindly at the ceiling for some-time. Nothing to see on the ceiling. Not even dust motes. The room was darker than a cave, with only flashes of white, blinding snow occasionally reflecting from a slit in the curtains.

He'd never had a woman respond to his lovemaking before with a case of insomnia and a fretful chewing on a thumbnail.

He wasn't sure whether to interpret her behavior as a killing blow to his masculine ego. Or a hopeful sign.

"You still awake?" he murmured.

Her slim white hand immediately shot under the blankets and laid still. "No, no, I was sleeping. I didn't wake you, did I?"

"The wind screaming in the eaves woke me." He found her hand under the cave of covers. Her fingers were ice-cold. Cold with anxiety, he mused, and guilt rumbled in his conscience in response.

He'd pushed her into making love, knowing she had some unspoken fears about passion and sex. Fears, maybe, about any situation where she could lose control, stemming from that teenage boy that she somehow still felt responsible for.

It raked against his ethical grain to ever push a lady, but he was fast running out of time and chances to be with her, much less woo her. Before tonight, he knew she had captured his heart. Before, he knew he was tumbling deep into love with her. And before, he had come to believe they belonged together, really belonged, not for some damn fool single night but for the long, lonely life haul. She was his match. His missing half.

And he'd hoped making love would help her reach the same conclusion. Surely she had seen the truth? The night had been unforgettable. She'd given, not like a yielding, but like an outpouring of emotions that had been trapped inside her forever. She'd come apart for him, like a flower opening for a life-giving drench of rain. She'd made him reel, the way no woman had made him reel. If she didn't realize that she had given him her complete trust, he did.

If it were his choice, she'd never leave his bed.

If it were his choice, for damn sure, she'd never leave his life.

"Stefan...?"

He heard the anxiety in her voice, and understood she wanted to talk. In principle, he believed whatever specific worry had her gnawing on that thumbnail needed to come out. But not quite yet. His fingertip traced the line of her jaw. "Did I tell you how beautiful you are, lambchop?"

"Yes."

The flush of heat skating up her long white throat delighted him. "Did I tell you how much I value the gift you gave me, that no one ever moved me as you do, that I love your nose, your toes, your knees and that exquisite tiny mole on your fann—"

"Yes."

More heat, more curling nerves—all in her eyes now. "And did I tell you that I love you, *lyubeesh?*"

"Stefan...you don't love me."

Her denial was immediate, her voice a whispered rush. So there, he mused, was the source of all that anxious fingernail chewing. "No?"

With his arms pinning her close, she couldn't skitter away from him, but her eyes shifted, bolting away like a nervous colt. "I don't know what happened tonight. I can't explain it. I've never just..." A white hand showed up over the covers, making some gesture that apparently was supposed to talk for her. "For heaven's sake, I never ripped off a man's clothes in my entire life."

"Perhaps," he said gravely, "this is a difference in perspective. Speaking from my shoes, I could not be more thrilled you chose to vent this particular impulse on me."

"Don't tease."

"Okeydoke, my toots, no more teasing. We are...um...suffering guilt, I take it? Not to worry. I can get into this. Russians are born with angst. Working up a good brooding guilt is an inbred specialty. Russians love suffering." Deliberately he hesitated. "But I am not exactly sure what we are suffering for?"

"You wretch. You're trying to make me laugh." Her fingers curled in his beard, tugged. For a moment there was humor in her eyes—exactly what he'd intended—but it didn't last. "Be serious with me, Stefan," she said quietly.

"Okay. No kidding now, tiger. I am listening." Beneath the covers, his hand slowly skimmed down her side, the caress both protective and possessive. He *was* listening. But Paige was always more rattled when he touched her. And she was predictably more honest when she was rattled.

"I don't know what you want. What you expect now."

"Hmm. We invited chaos, and now you're afraid there is a price to pay."

"Yes. Exactly. One of these weeks, you're going to move on. You only temporarily set up here, to get your bearings until you made up your mind about a job."

"There is no university here," he agreed, "and I must make up my mind about a job fairly soon."

"I understand. But my home is here. A home that matters to me. When my parents retired to Arizona, they wanted to sell the house and really raised hell with me about staying in the rattling old place alone. But there've been Stanfords there since the 1700s. It's our roots, our family home base, the source of all the family history. I just can't give it up.''

He wondered if she expected him to buy this red herring. Paige valued truth as fiercely as he did, and God knew there was honesty in her eyes. But he already knew that she had strong emotional and loyalty ties to her family and that house. And her bringing this up at all revealed that a future together had been on her mind, including the problem of where they might live. ''Did you think I would ask you to give up your home?'' he asked her.

She touched his cheek. ''I don't know. But it's not just that. I can't see you happy with a fling, Stefan, something short-term, something with no ties. From everything you've told me about your life, you just never take that road. No matter how tough the odds have been, you've never settled for anything less than what really mattered to you.''

''Loyalty and commitment are values I can't shake,'' he admitted. ''A fling is for boys. A waste of time, a waste of heart. You could not be more right, toots. I want it all or nothing—a woman who is willing to take all the risks with me, as I am with her.''

He'd expressed his heart before; none of this was headline news. Yet her eyes responded as if she'd been punched. He saw her swallow. Felt her whole body go still. ''That's what I'm trying to be honest about, Stefan. I can't be that risk taker you want. In the long-term, I just don't think we'd work. I'm too cautious and careful and too much a boring plodder by nature.''

Stefan considered pulling out the hairs in his beard. In painful tufts. Her voice was so earnest, her gaze so sincerely troubled. Yet her self-perceptions were so opposite to what he knew of her that they were crazy. His so-careful lover had taken every naked risk with him there was. His so-cautious lady had been compellingly wild and free when she was in his arms. His so-boring plodder had so much rich sensuality and passion inherent in her nature that it poured from her like a river. And in her life, she had chosen a career path and life-style that showed guts and strength, marching to no one else's drummer. "You think of yourself as cautious." He echoed her blankly.

"I *have* to be, Stefan." She took a breath. "When I was a kid, no one expected me to amount to anything. I was on a fast track downhill, a rebel with any excuse for a cause, a black sheep in the making. My parents, my family and background were wonderful—there was no *reason* for my being so awful."

"Awful," he repeated.

"It stemmed from hormones then. I acted on impulse. Leaped into every situation blindly, selfishly. Stefan, I hurt people."

"Cookie," he said quietly, "that was many years ago. And if there is a soul who can escape living without hurting someone, I have yet to meet them."

"I don't want to hurt you!"

"And you are so sure you will?"

"I'm sure that my behavior tonight wasn't me. I'm sure that you're in a strange, new place and right in the middle of changing your whole life. I think that loneliness could easily be affecting your feelings for me. And if we become too attached, you'll be hurt."

There was nothing in this he could argue. His life *was* in the process of upheaval; he could not claim to be settled. If this was the nature of chaos she feared, though, it had never shown up in her behavior, her touch, her eyes.

She had yet to tell him that she didn't love him, didn't care—or that she was afraid of being hurt herself. A fear of hurting him seemed to trouble her far more, adding a deeper spin on the problem he hadn't considered before. Somehow the incident with that teenage boy seemed to have convinced her that she was responsible for protecting others from her wicked, wicked ways. She could not hurt anyone else if she were cold, if she were a good girl, if she never let loose a hormone or a desire, never laughed too loud or cried too hard. That she was trying to shut herself off from all the riches of life and experience did not seem to occur to her.

Stefan certainly recognized there was a level where her fear was real. She could hurt him. Badly. Maybe irrevocably. But he could lose the chance for a life-long soul mate if he didn't take the risk.

And somehow, someway, he needed to show her that certain risks were the only ones in heaven or hell worth taking.

"So," he said slowly, "you think we should fight this attachment?"

"I think we should be reasonable. And careful. Especially careful to be truthful with each other."

"Truthful with each other." His tongue wrapped around that word. "Yes. I promise you, fiercely promise you, my lambchop, that I will never be less than honest with you."

There. That was all he had to say to see the rage of relief in her eyes. Her whole body relaxed. Her soft mouth curved, almost turned into a smile...

Until he swept her beneath him.

When Paige pushed open the front door, she felt like a stranger walking into her own house. The answering machine was blinking. Three days of newspapers and mail had accumulated, three days of fresh dust. Whole intimate parts of her body were tender and self-aware, and she hadn't even come home for fresh clothes in the past seventy-two hours.

She hadn't needed clothes. Fresh or otherwise. Maybe an alcoholic after a binge had memory blackouts like this, only she hadn't had a drink. Even a sip of wine. And though she was confoundly confused how the past three days had happened, certain memories were crystal, indelibly clear. She'd made love with Stefan by the fire in his living room, in his bed, on the kitchen counter. They'd christened almost every room in his house and certainly his navy blue couch. They'd nearly killed themselves in the bathtub, but that hadn't stopped them, either. Nothing had stopped Stefan.

Or her.

She pushed off her jacket, hung it on a hook on the wall tree, tossed her hat and gloves on the closet shelf, struggling to convince herself that she hadn't gone stark, raving insane. Maybe at some level her behavior was understandable. Maybe if you'd been buttoned up for a dozen years, the kiss of a prince was always going to bring on a spell of enchantment.

It was just damn terrifying that she couldn't seem to make herself wake up from it. Not for three long days.

And not now, even though she was home, and everything around her was mundane and normal and comfortingly real-life.

She'd left Stefan napping on the couch. Years ago, she'd shaken smoking, beat her chocoholic craving, and licked her lead-foot-on-the-accelerator habit. If she just removed herself from the damn Russian's presence, she could surely shake his hold on her, too.

The telephone jangled just as she was crossing the hall. She snatched the receiver before it could scream in her ear a second time. She recognized her sister's voice. Gwen, no different than Abby, rarely wasted time on a greeting before starting in.

"He'd better have offered you a ring before sleeping with you, or I'm flying there and punching him right in the nose. And you can take that promise right to the bank."

Paige sank onto the third stair. Perhaps she'd been precipitate in her previous opinion. She was hungry for her work, for her cameos and that whole side of real life. But lingering in fantasyland would be a lot easier than dealing with her sisters. Either of her sisters. "I beg your pardon? Did I miss a hello and how are you in this conversation?"

"You slept with him, didn't you?"

"Is there a reason on earth you would suddenly leap to this extraordinary imaginative conclusion?"

"Of course there is. You haven't answered your phone in days—"

"You *know* I don't always answer the phone when I get busy with work."

"But you always quit working by nine, which is why we've always called each other at night. So if you didn't answer, you weren't there. And if you didn't tell either Abby or me where you were going, that means you didn't want us to know. So you were with that guy. That neighbor.'' Gwen stopped to yell something to the boys. Regretfully it didn't break her concentration. "Abby's thrilled spitless you finally found a man to push your buttons, but Abby would never let a man interfere with her career or her life. She isn't you. So don't listen to her advice, listen to mine. Don't you mess with anyone just because he has a bucket of charm."

"Yes, Gwen."

"Don't you fool around unless he's serious. A guy who's looking for a little excitement on the side can really mess with your mind. Believe me, I know.''

"Yes, Gwen."

"I'm not giving you mom's lecture on morality. I don't care about morality. I'm talking about you. You never could take anything light. Every cause with you was always heart and soul. And this guy'd better value that or I'm gonna kill him."

"Yes, Gwen."

"So. How was the sex?"

Paige rolled her eyes. All those "Yes, Gwens" hadn't gained her an inch. You could tell a stranger, a mom, a best friend—anyone on earth—to mind their own business. There was just no purpose in trying to tell a sister. At least one of *her* sisters. "Hey. I haven't admitted to doing anything yet," she said dryly.

Gwen hadn't been labeled the bulldog in the family for nothing. "Just tell me how it was on a scale of one to ten. Ten being Mel Gibson, and one being folding laundry would have been more fun."

"If I tell you it was a fifty-seven, would you quit prying?"

"Fifty-seven? Hot spit and holy horsefeathers."
The receiver creaked. A door slammed. And then all
background noises emanating from her sister's house
in St. Augustine abruptly died. "Maybe I'd better fly
home. If he's that potent a package, I don't trust your
judgment. I think Abby and I should get a look at
him, and if you need protection—"

"If either of you show up here, you die." Paige
rubbed two fingers on her temples. Maybe she never
intended to let that fifty-seven slip out, but it certainly served to divert Gwen from her own problems.
And that was good. Her sister had always been meant
to mother a small planet. She thrived on being needed.
Only Paige was well aware that her sisters were more
than capable of arriving and playing Mounties, because tarnation, she'd leap in to interfere and rescue
them the same way. "I was joking," she said firmly.
"Just trying to make you laugh. I've been busy with
work. That's all that's going on."

"You never could lie worth peas. Dammit. I *knew*
you were in trouble. You're in love with him?"

Paige squeezed her eyes closed. "Hey. You haven't
said one word about how my two hellion nephews are
doing. Or your job. Or how things are going with your
ex . . ."

Gwen wasn't easily put off. When it came to the care
and maintenance of family, neither of her sisters were
easily derailed. But sisters or no sisters, Paige wasn't
ready to share anything about Stefan yet. Her emotions for him were too turbulent and confused and way
too private.

As soon as she hung up, she bounded up the stairs
to change clothes. She needed to work. Now. She
hadn't touched a tool or a cameo in three days, which

seemed impossible. Work was never off her mind. Her whole life was boundaried by the rigid discipline and concentration she counted on in her work.

In her room, she peeled off clothes and scrambled around for fresh jeans, a sweatshirt, socks. It was only by accident that she caught her reflection in the dresser mirror.

A stranger stared back. It wasn't her. The plain white bra and utilitarian panties were familiar. So was the same old ordinary body. But the woman in the mirror had a long, loose cascade of hair streaming down her back. Stefan had lost her hairpins, claimed he couldn't find a rubber band in his whole house to hold a braid together. Stefan had put those beard-blushes on her skin, too. But it was more than the marks of loving or wantonly streaming hair that made her reflection look different.

Her eyes were soft. Softer than dreams. Her skin had a flush that refused to go away. Her mouth looked shamelessly vulnerable. The woman in the mirror had just come from the bed of a lover—a lover who'd up-ended her whole world—and it showed. When she lifted her hands, she discovered them trembling.

She yanked on socks. Sweatshirt. Jeans. She was supposed to be a tough, strong, self-reliant, self-sufficient, sturdy New England woman. Not a trembler.

Likely it was guilt making her tremble. Anytime, over the past three days, she could have said no. Stefan had never once forced her, never even really seduced her. She had wanted him. Endlessly. Powerfully. Beyond reason, beyond any compelling force that she had ever dreamed of.

Do you love him, Gwen had asked her.

An unbearably unfair question. That damn Russian had owned her heart, probably from the day he'd put out the fire in her kitchen and started one in her emotions. If she didn't love him, she could dismiss the past three days as the crazed but understandable behavior of a sex-starved spinster. If she hadn't fallen head over sinking, drowning heels, she would never have worried about how badly he could get hurt.

It was a worry she couldn't shake. A boy had died, the one time in her life when she'd been wildly irresponsible. When anyone let hormones rule their life, someone was bound to get hurt. Hormones made people blind. Maybe that was human, but Paige had been too damn human once. And the only way she had learned to forgive herself was being sure—damn sure—she'd changed.

Outside, the snowstorm had long died. The February sun was stunningly bright. Icicles hung from the eaves, dripping rainbows. Those prisms of color shot off the walls and glowed on the jade cameo on her dresser.

She stared at the carved profile of the woman, no different than she had, a dozen times. Until these past three days with Stefan, she could have sworn there was nothing similar between that sensually abandoned woman and herself. Now she felt frightened. All this time, she thought she *knew* herself. All this time, she'd been so sure of what mattered to her, sure of who she was, sure of what a good woman was. The woman she *wanted* to be.

Be honest with yourself, her mind counseled her. But she had always been ruthlessly honest with herself. Truth guided everything she did—even her work. Every time she carved a cameo, she was driven by the age-old sculpting principle that the artist could not create truth. The truth was always there; her job was only to carve away what wasn't the truth.

Yet if she carved away what couldn't be…she came up with her and Stefan. He was so strong. A man of unbendable ideals and unshakable values. He never made a secret of what he wanted and needed from a woman. He wanted it all. A woman's heart, soul, body, and total loyalty. A woman who could give with no holds barred. A woman who could embrace life with the same exuberance and joy and whole heart that he did.

Paige could wish to be that woman for Stefan all day long, but her fear of failing him seemed an insolvable problem. And wishing alone wouldn't give her courage and confidence she simply didn't have.

She could not carve beauty into a cameo if that beauty wasn't already inherent in the stone. This was no different. She could not make herself into a woman who wasn't there.

Feeling a thick, hard lump well in her throat, she picked up the jade cameo and carried it downstairs. Heaven knew why she'd postponed making the decision that she should have made weeks ago.

She'd send it to Harry.

He'd sell it.

And she'd be rid of it.

Ten

"Stefan, you went to so much trouble! You never had to do this."

"Well, of course I did. You finished the cameo. Clearly a celebration was called for." Stefan had carried the coral cameo she'd made for her sister out of the shop. Flanked by two candles, it made the centerpiece on their dinner table.

Paige's work on the cameo had kept her too busy to see him for the past several days. He understood that certain work took intense concentration. He understood that there were certain stages in a project when it was utterly frustrating to be interrupted.

He understood, perfectly well, that she'd been avoiding him as zealously as a cat hid from a pending thunderstorm.

"Paige..." He motioned to the cameo again. "I

really don't know how you did this, but I can't tell you enough times—it's beyond beautiful."

Her gaze strayed to the cameo, too—in between bites of dinner. It had taken him three trips from the car to cart in the whole feast. He'd promised her a sampling of Russian foods weeks ago. She'd been wary and suspicious of the first course—red caviar, mounded on crackers and served with champagne— but her eyes lit up after the first taste. The Ukrainian borscht had not gone over so well. After one spoonful, he'd seen the unforgettable expression on her face—and whisked the bowl out of sight. Beet soup was clearly never going to be her cuppa.

She was diving into the shashlik—broiled lamb— now. No avalanche or runaway train, he mused, had better get between his lady and her food when she loved something. And as long as the conversation stayed within the boundaries of food or her work, she was easy and relaxed with him.

"I never know how any cameo is going to turn out." Her left hand reached out to trace a fingertip on the cameo's profile. "But I have to admit, I'm pleased with this. Gwen's birthday is a couple of months away yet. I built in enough time to start over if I didn't like how this project worked out, but in the strangest way, this just couldn't be more perfect for her."

"How so?" His praise had come from the heart. He really didn't know how she'd done it. Somehow there seemed to be two women in the coral. One was a profile of a woman with short-cropped hair and delicate cheekbones, whose face was set in a grave expression. Behind her—it almost seemed as if it were a trick of light—the same woman with the short-cropped hair was profiled in the darker shade of coral, but she was laughing, happy, her face tilted to the sun.

"Well . . . the way it turned out . . . it's like there's a shadow of the real woman hiding in the background. You see?" When Stefan nodded, Paige struggled to explain. "That's so like my sister. Gwen doesn't see herself as beautiful. She's always so busy, always does so much for other people, that it's like she's never had time to really look at herself."

Maybe that applied to her sister, but Stefan thought his own lady fit that shadow idea, too. Paige had hidden parts of her personality for years, buried needs and feelings out of sight. So typically, she was wearing a voluminous sweatshirt that concealed every feminine curve. A tightly woven braid concealed a waterfall of rich, lustrously thick hair that caught a thousand points of light when let loose. It was too late to hide such things from him.

He'd heard her laughter pealing free. He'd seen her eyes darken with desire, her face naked with vulnerability. He'd seen, felt, touched every inch of her skin. He knew her giving nature and the huge wealth of emotions in her heart.

Pretty damn clear he knew too much, because as fast as he'd told her he loved her, Paige had buried herself behind an answering machine and judicious, defensive and inarguably justified excuses such as work.

Food, temporarily, had brought her out of hiding.

Stefan served her two more dishes. He'd been considering the problem for several days now. Food was good. Food was effective. Food was a pretty damn helpful method of tempting Paige, but it wasn't getting the job done. This particular kitten was ready to bolt at the first sign of lightning. Nothing he'd done yet had lessened her fear of thunderstorms one iota.

He was losing right now, and knew it. For a man who'd never backed down from risk, who had followed his heart and conscience no matter what prices he'd had to pay, Stefan could not remember being this scared. Either he gambled for the whole pot, or Paige might never budge past go.

"What's this?" she asked.

"*Vatrushka.* A kind of cheese pastry." He set the dishes in front of her. "And the small thin pancakes with jam are called *blinchikis.* Is disgracefully unbalanced meal, I know. But I just wanted to give you a whole range of Russian foods to sample."

"Oh, God. Oh, God. How many of these *blinchikis* did you make?"

From the look in her eyes, not enough. If there was ever going to be a good time to pull off a bluff, this was it. "I thought a lot about what you said," he mentioned casually.

"Hmm?" She had a mouthful of *blinchikis,* which she swallowed quickly. "About what?"

"You were simply right, toots. About the two of us needing to cool down. I'm not settled, not financially secure, not nothing. If I were a woman, I'd put a relationship with such a man on a back furnace."

"Back burner." She corrected him gently. But for the first time since her tongue discovered those *blinchikis,* her eyes were on his, straight on his, instead of on the food.

He'd fed her food before. Now he fed her what she'd claimed—always claimed—to want to hear. "The more I thought about it, the more I think it would be totally unfair to complicate your life . . . to

complicate either of our lives...right now." He
watched her pick up a forkful of *blinchikis*. The fork
stalled midair. She seemed to have forgotten it. "It was
what you said all along, yes, that it would be best to
be friends? Just not a good time to pursue more. Not
a good time to invite chaos, so to speak."

"Yes. Exactly." She repeated, "Exactly."

He expected to see relief in her eyes. He was the
same as promising the kitten that she never had to face
thunder and lightning, never even had to risk getting
her paws wet. But there was a sudden stricken still-
ness in her face. And when the piece of *blinchinki* fell
off her fork, she didn't seem to notice. Stefan swallowed acid. He'd never gone for broke on a bluff before, but either a man played for the whole pot or
nothing. "By the way, I have pinned down job."

"I..." She dropped the fork altogether. And then
smiled. Brilliantly. "That's wonderful news! Tell me
all about it. Where's the job?"

"Well, originally I had offers from several places.
MIT. Yale. Berkeley. California pretty damn hot. The
other two...I think they are great places, with great
people, but they both seemed a little stuffed in the lip."

"I think you mean 'stiff upper lip,'" Paige said
gently.

"Whatever. There was a...properness...in their
discussions with me. I was unsure if I would fit in. I
can put on a tie but my nature is a small bit on the exuberant, boisterous side. Almost sure, actually low-
down dead sure, that they would not like me."

"Stefan! They would love you! Anyone would love
you, you doofus!"

"Doofus? This is a word I haven't heard before."

"It's an insult," she informed him. "Particularly useful when you're trying to scold someone."

Perhaps, he thought. But if he'd offered her a Godiva chocolate, he doubted she could leap to his defense faster. And whatever this "doofus" really meant, he heard the way she said the word and saw the fire of loyalty in her eyes. She could insult him all day this way if she wanted. "Anyway. Weeks ago, I decided to look at other schools, universities closer to here. I called a few up, talked to a few deans. Unfortunately, I am a complicated person to hire, because I am not a full-fledged American citizen yet. But I looked at Bennington, Middlebury, and Dartmouth just over the border in New Hampshire."

"All terrific schools."

"Middlebury is the closest." He added carefully, deliberately, "But still not commuting distance from here."

"Way too far to commute," she agreed swiftly.

"But it does seem they don't starve their professors. A house comes with the job. A ton of complicated paperwork would have to be worked out. And they pushed pretty hard for a decision. They'd want me there by mid-March."

"Mid-March?" Her fork clattered to the floor. She never even glanced at it. "But that's only a few weeks away."

"Uh-huh. I think they sense fish on the line. Better reel in, before I have time to consider other opportunities. I believe they are hot to expand their physics program. The dean in the physics department was pretty low-down excited. Good man. We were talking the same language so quickly it was like we were old friends. And fish or no fish, the timing would work well.'' Stefan only had one more card to play. ''I only rented the house from Jasper until the end of March. I have no reason to think he would mind extending the lease, but that was the original time frame deal.''

''You never told me that before.'' Her elbow collided with a wineglass. It almost toppled. ''I mean... I knew you were only here temporarily, but I had no idea you had to move so soon.''

He raised his eyebrows. ''It was no secret. I would have told you. You never asked. Now... what can I serve you more?''

''Heavens, nothing. I couldn't eat another bite. Dinner was beyond splendiferous... but very filling.''

''Da. Russian cooking is heavy. So heavy it would give anyone a justifiable excuse for a lazy nap after dinner.''

''You can say that again—''

''But I have a much better solution for that problem.'' Maybe it was his teasing tone that made her cheeks suddenly flush, but Stefan suspected he knew what crossed her mind. She thought his solution was to whisk her off to bed.

Heaven knew, he wanted to.

Instead he surged out of his chair and disappeared into the hall. Seconds later, he came back, holding her jacket, gloves and boots. She shook her head violently. He nodded just as violently. ''Fresh air great cure for full stomach,'' he said coaxingly.

''Forget it, you bully. I like the nap idea much, much better. I'm all comfortable and warm and full. It's *cold* out there. And dark. Hey, you—come back here and argue with me—''

He emerged from the hall again, this time carrying his jacket and boots. "I have yet to make a snowman. This is a sacred American custom, isn't it?"

"It's a *daylight* custom."

"How can you be American and not know the Sinatra song? When you're American, you can sometimes revise the rules and do it *your* way."

"No. No, no, no. This is insane, Michaelovich. Not a little insane. This is big-time crazy—"

She loved crazy. Stefan could never fathom why she didn't realize it. She thrived on impulse, on fun, on laughter. She came alive and turned on like a ray of fresh sunshine. She was so happy by nature—when she let herself be.

He not only wanted her happy, but temporarily he wanted her too busy to dwell on the whole previous conversation. So he argued with her, and bullied her into trundling up, and dragged her outside to make a snowman by moonlight. She protested the whole time at this childish enterprise . . . but she packed the first snowball, perfect and round, before rolling it in the fresh powder of her backyard.

The night was bitter-biting freezing. No wind, but the exquisite and beautiful shower of moonlight wasn't worth an ounce of warmth. The snowman project kept her far too busy to think, and the cold kept her far too busy to stand still long enough to even consider thinking—at least about serious problems.

They argued, long and loudly, about theory. He just wanted a plain old roly-poly American snowman. But Paige was an artist, and incapable of leaving it at that. Stacking a trio of round snowballs didn't begin to cut her mustard. She wanted a Russian snowman, and she wanted him fancy. Towering tall with a cossack hat.

Pinecones for buttons. She poked itsy twigs into his chin to give him whiskers, then chased around the yard to find something brown she could use to give him thick, brooding eyebrows. Still, she wasn't done. *Somewhere* there was a bush with red winter berries that she claimed would be ideal for his cheeks and mouth.

Hells bells, the woman would have played all night. By then her fingers and toes had to be threatening frostbite. His were. The same way he'd hustled and conned her into going out, he now had to bully and cajole her into heading inside again.

He herded her as far as the door—and Paige even opened it—but then she whisked around again, standing with the yellow pool of warm light behind her, determined to get one more look at their snowman. "He's beautiful," she announced. "A prize-winner. Conceivably the most unforgettable snowman that has ever been created in the history of time."

So was she—unforgettable—when she tipped her face to his. Her hat was crusted with snow, her gloves caked solid. Snow was melting, glittering in her short eyelashes like miniature diamonds. Her cheeks were as red as flame, and so was her moist, red mouth.

He reached for her—awkwardly, because his gloved hands, too, were numb and snow-caked. And his mouth was as icy cold as hers when their lips first connected.

It was in her eyes, that she expected him to come in, expected they would warm each other by making love. He hadn't touched her in days now, but her eyes were liquid with the memories of when he had. No matter what fears or objections she built up in her mind, the power of her heart had overcome them before. Her heart had already said yes.

He kissed her hard, fast, fiercely. Desperately, if she only knew. A man who'd deliberately gotten a woman chilled was honor bound to warm her, and yet a kiss that started rough and wild turned slow and quiet. Moonlight quiet. Crystal-clear night quiet. Soul quiet, except for her sudden rushed breathing. And his.

He lifted his head, his gaze sweeping over her face. Her soft mouth was unsteady, her skin vulnerably flushed. The naked yearning in her eyes, though, turned uneasy when he continued to say nothing and failed to smile. She was used to smiles from him. As she should be. His nature had always been to snatch every ounce of happiness and laughter he could wrench from life, and it had become his nature to share it. With her.

It was an unbearably frightening risk, to give her exactly what she'd asked him for. He was leaving, disappearing from her life soon, and she would no longer have to worry about him causing her problems in any way. While they were romping in the snow, he hadn't wanted to give her time to think about that.

But as he turned around and left her, he hoped, he violently hoped, that she took plenty of time to think about it now. Paige had to decide what mattered to her. There was no forcing love. She was the only one who could define the nature of love and loyalty in her own heart.

From the den window, Paige could see the lumpy blob their snowman had melted into. The yard was no longer pristine white, but slushy-mucky soup, and typical of March, a wild, screaming wind had howled incessantly all day. The wind rattled the eaves and made her nerves rattle right along with it.

She wasn't exactly sure when February had sneaked into March, but the lion winds kept roaring in her mind as if it were a reminder that Stefan was leaving.

Soon. Very soon now.

"Cookie, could you define 'cruel and unusual punishment' for me?"

"No. Not now." *Star Trek* was showing one of the priceless episodes with Q, but neither of them turned on the tube. Stefan had asked her if she'd mind looking over the forms involved in all his citizen papers. She'd said sure. He'd brought over some history tomes to keep himself occupied while she studied the forms. So far the history tomes weren't keeping him busy. And nothing was keeping him quiet.

"Well, I have a serious question about the freedom of religion. I mean . . . what if someone has religious beliefs about using drugs? Or about conducting services in the nude? If it is actually someone's religion—even if those beliefs could cause medical or personal harm or offend others—this is really still okay?"

"Button it, Stefan. I'm onto you. You already know ten times more about the constitution than any American I ever met. You don't need me to help you interpret a damn thing—you just love discussing that stuff. And I do, too, but I can't concentrate on these papers if you keep *talking* to me. Now if you say one more word—even one teensy-weensy tiny word—I am going to strangle you with pillows until you are dead, dead, dead."

"Hmm. Is there any chance this means you don't want to explain 'probable cause' right this minute?"

She hurled a tapestry pillow toward his face at torpedo speed. Since he was only sitting on the other side of the couch, the pillow easily had enough momentum to thwack him good. He made an *oomph* sound when it collided, but when he lifted off the pillow, his grin was exasperatingly male, unrepentant and irrepressible.

"I'll be good," he vowed.

"I'll only believe that if I can get it in blood, duckie."

"Get it in blood?"

"A slang phrase. A blood promise means you really mean it. And the 'duckie' was just your simple, basic American insult. Although trying to insult you is like trying to get through cement, in your case."

"Aaah."

Another mischievous grin. She responded by rolling her eyes—and pointing her finger toward the door. "That's it. I've had it with you, you big nuisance. Out, out, out."

"You're throwing me out?" His tone sounded injured, and he hammed up his hurt feelings by covering his heart with a big, splayed hand.

"You bet your sweet bippy I am. Go walk around. Go raid the fridge. Go do whatever you have to do to vent some of that physical energy. Just give me fifteen minutes of solid quiet to wade through this stuff."

"Okeydoke, my darling."

Paige ignored that "darling" and forced her attention to the sea of papers, which were strewn every which way from her lap to the floor. She had no idea so much was involved in becoming a U.S. citizen. Stefan had a lawyer. He hadn't asked for or expected her help at any legal level, but nothing in the American language had prepared him for legalese. He was just hoping she might be able to translate some of the forms, but there seemed to be a million of them—all in triplicate—involving terms like "work authorization" and "petitioner letters" and "diversity visas." She had to study a mountain to even have a clue what those terms meant.

Absently her fingers reached up to stroke the cameo at her throat. The cameo happened to be an old-fashioned garbo—meaning oval-shaped—and was the first one she'd made from a cowrie shell. The cameo was pinned to a high-necked ivory blouse with a flutter of lace, and paired with a longish camel skirt. Nothing formal or fancy, but it wasn't as if there was a *rule* she had to wear jeans every day. She'd just felt like wearing a skirt. She'd just felt like putting on a little blush, and Shalimar, and for no reason at all had just been in a mood to leave her hair down.

Stefan hadn't seemed to notice. Not the hair down, not the cameo, not the skirt. It didn't hurt, she told herself. For days now, they'd had a great time together, bickering and talking and treating each other as if they were brother and sister. She was thrilled, downright thrilled, that he'd cooled down. It was good he was leaving. Good for him, good for her. Their attachment had been too intense, too dangerous, too begging-for-heartbreak risky.

But damn if her heart wasn't breaking. Breaking like silver splinters, fragile, sharp, causing an aching pain that she couldn't seem to shake. A good woman, she'd told herself a thousand times, had the will-power and character to do what was right and ignore something stupid and unbearable like heartbreak.

It was safer this way. When he got himself established, settled down, she had no doubt that a ton of women would come flocking. He would not be lonely for long. He'd find the right woman, someone who matched him in courage and spirit. She could never have lived with herself if she failed Stefan, and she'd always believed that she only appealed to him because he was alone and she was convenient.

Convenient.

A phrase suddenly leaped out of her from the sea of papers. Cripes, they were a mess. Files five and six inches thick. Tons of legalese, and she'd had to wade through the whole first batch before understanding that Stefan had something called a Diversity Visa. Apparently this special type of visa was made possible through the Immigration Act of 1990, which opened the country's doors to certain people with extraordinary skills or education. It was no surprise to Paige that Stefan had easily been singled out as uniquely valuable.

She could have told 'em that without his having to fill out all those blasted forms.

Still. Getting in and staying in were two different issues. Paige waded through more files, slowly picking up the rules and complications involved in his becoming a naturalized citizen. The surest route was if the immigrant applying for citizenship had a U.S. relative to sponsor him—but no blood relationship except for father and brother applied. His distant cousins couldn't help him there.

She only found one other sure way. Her gaze leaped to the page she had clenched in her left hand. Minutes before, the phrase had drawn her attention like a magnet. It was just a set of words. ''If married to a

U.S. citizen, the spouse can petition on the alien's behalf..."

A lump filled her throat as she read further. Every paragraph and clause made the issue clearer. If he were married—or chose to marry—an American, his bid for naturalized citizenship would not only be faster, but be about guaranteed.

It would really be "convenient" for him to have an American wife.

Paige strongly suspected that Stefan knew that. This whole mound of files was partly a measure of how fiercely he wanted to become an American. She couldn't help but think of all the emotional and personal prices Stefan had paid to come here. And he had a long history of doing whatever he had to, when a goal that really mattered to him was at stake.

"Hey."

She swallowed quickly, painfully, when she heard his voice. And looked up.

"I was going to be good and not interrupt you—this is truth, I swear! But I wandered into your workroom. I didn't see your jade cameo and I wondered what happened to it."

"You're right. It's gone. I packed it up last week and mailed it to Harry...he's the man who markets all my stuff. I'm pretty sure I told you about him before—"

Stefan stepped into the room. "You mean it's on its way to be sold?"

"Yup."

"You would give away the jade?" he asked disbelievingly.

He made it sound as though she was giving away something precious. She had no way to explain that she simply needed it out of her sight. She was twenty-seven, old enough to live her life based on principles and truth. And way too old to believe in fairy tales or dreams that couldn't be.

"Paige, I . . ." It was impossible to miss the dark, brooding frown carved on his forehead, and there was pain in his eyes—the sharp, lancing pain of despair—that she didn't understand. She assumed he was about to tell her what was bothering him, but then never had the chance to find out.

The doorbell rang, interrupting them both.

Nothing could have startled her more than to find her sister Abby on the front porch.

Eleven

They'd taken off on her. Both the turkeys. Paige would have blamed her sister—Abby was so used to functioning in the cutthroat business world that she was pretty skilled at manipulating men. Only nothing and no one could manipulate Stefan, and he hadn't needed any persuading to take off. The pair of them had taken one look at each other, sized the other up and mutually stampeded for their coats. As if they were reading from the same cue card, they'd even babbled out the same excuse—poor Paige had been working all day, so it struck them both as a great idea to head for town and pick up a nice, easy takeout dinner while she relaxed.

Dinner, her foot.

Paige was chewing on a thumbnail when she finally heard the front doorknob turn an hour later. Her sister jogged in, carrying sacks of Chinese—enough for ten marines—but noticeably alone.

"What'd you do with Stefan?"

"Took him home. He didn't mind, not once I explained that I only had a few hours with you. My plane leaves at nine tomorrow morning—I've got a business meeting at three I can't miss. He can see you any old time. I've only got tonight."

Paige shook her head. "Tell me you didn't fly all the way here for less than a twenty-four-hour visit."

"I sure as hell did. Gwen couldn't. She doesn't have the money, and what would she do with our two hellion nephews while she was gone? But we both decided it was time one of us got a look at your guy."

"Did it occur to either of you that if I'd wanted your interference, I'd have asked for it?"

Abby raised her eyebrows. "Of course it did. What does that have to do with anything? We're your sisters. Stefan understood that with no sweat at all, so don't have a cow."

"You *told* Stefan you wanted to look him over?"

"Sure. I grilled him up the wazoo. Trust me, he didn't mind."

"Maybe he didn't mind, but I'm mortified. If I had any cyanide in the medicine cabinet, I'd be gulping it right now. You probably embarrassed him to death. *And* me. Dammit, Abby, you should have talked to me before doing anything like this."

"If you thought Gwen or I were in trouble, you'd just sit on the sidelines and do nothing, huh?"

"That's an entirely different thing."

"I know. Gwen and I are both reasonably subtle. You'd probably show up with six guns ablazing."

"I don't own a gun."

"A moot point. Words, guns, billy clubs...we all have our favorite choice of weapons. You're our baby sister. And Gwen was getting an ulcer worrying about you. And I don't think it'd kill any guy to discover you have family who love you."

"I don't love you. I'm so mad at you I could strangle you with my bare hands. And I may."

"After dinner," Abby advised. "Fighting is lousy on digestion. We can pick up this fight right after we finish the Chinese, okay?"

They didn't pick up the fight right after dinner. Abby leveled enough food for three women, and kept a running monologue on family news, her job, politics, PMS, how good it was to be home, Dad's health, hair, nails and the state of the world.

As soon as the dishes were done, Paige grabbed the phone to call Stefan—he'd left all his citizenship papers in her den—but Abby stopped her. "He knows they're here, because he mentioned it. In fact he mentioned several things about his citizenship status. He said not to worry, he'd just pick up the papers later when he had the chance," she said cheerfully, and then more quietly, "You're not even going to ask what I thought of him, are you?"

"No."

"No," Abby murmured, "You're that far gone that you don't give a damn what anyone thinks, do you...you know exactly where your heart stands on that man."

By then, Abby had pushed off her spectator pumps and slipped out of her suit jacket. It didn't matter how relaxed she was. Paige always figured that if her sister were stark naked in a shower, she'd still look dressed for success. The navy blue suit, the scarf with the tasteful splash of color, the perfect makeup and hair-cut were only part of it. Abby had an attitude beneath the surface, a chin-high, dare-the-world confidence. She wore drive and determination as if it were a second skin. There wasn't a hint of vulnerability in anything about her physical appearance.

But Paige saw the faint lines of strain around her sister's eyes, the restlessness. There was a fragility she sensed in Abby, even if it didn't show. "You're not happy," she said worriedly.

Abby dismissed her concern faster than the speed of sound. "Sure I am. Everything couldn't be going better."

"Did you get that promotion?"

"I won't know for a few more weeks." Her eyes flashed a grin. "That promotion is a battle, but I've always had to fight for everything I won. For some people, that'd be stress. For me, that's what I am—a fighter. This is just one more war."

Maybe, Paige thought, but she still had the intuition that her sister was headed for a crisis. If she couldn't get Abby to talk further about her work, though, at least for a few hours she laid off the subject of Stefan.

They headed upstairs before ten. The spare beds weren't made up. Paige could have thrown on fresh sheets in her sister's old bedroom in a few seconds, but Abby insisted that fussing that way for one night seemed silly. It wasn't as though they'd never huddled together in Paige's old-fashioned four-poster before. Growing up, all three sisters had been scared of the dark. Paige's bed was the biggest, and a hundred times the three of them had sacked out together, buried in blankets, talking until the wee hours.

Her sister's visit was like going back in time. They bumped hips in the bathroom, bickering over sink space, talking ten for a dozen through all the nightly female rituals of face washing and brushing teeth and putting away clothes. Abby drew the curtains; Paige flicked off the lights. No different than when they were kids, they dived under the blankets and yelped at the freezing-cold sheets.

Gradually, though, the sheets warmed up, and their eyes became adjusted to the pitch-dark room. Both of them were studying the dust motes in the ceiling, not looking at each other, when Abby started talking again. Paige was already mentally braced. A bookie would never bother with odds on her sister forgetting the subject of Stefan entirely.

"He's adorable," Abby said thoughtfully.

"I know he is."

"Sexy. Smart. And a good man. I don't run into many good men, not in my line of work, so I recognized one of those rare breeds right away."

"He is. The rarest of good men."

Abby carefully picked her words. "But I think it has to be tough for a man to know how he really feels about anything, with so many changes going on in his life. Everybody moves. Everybody changes jobs. But he's doing it all at once—different job, different home, different country. That's a pretty big emotional uproar."

"Believe me, I've told myself those things a dozen times."

"It's just so damn easy to confuse loneliness for something else."

"I know."

Abby turned her head. "And I'm sure you realize how badly he wants to become an American."

"I know."

"Paige?"

"What?"

"I'm pretty sure you know this, too—that it'd be a hell of a lot easier for him to become an American with a U.S. wife. Not that it can't be done through other channels, but an American wife would make it a 'for sure.' He might not *mean* to. But he could be using you."

Paige closed her eyes. "I've considered that." All evening, the issue had nagged on her mind like a toothache. Stefan had specifically chosen to bring her all those legal papers—ostensibly to seek her help. Through the history of their relationship, though, he'd asked for her help a ton of times when he needed it like a hole in the head. And her Russian had to know she would run across that citizenship information about American wives.

Stefan never did anything without a purpose. And as much as she loved him, it was usually a sneaky purpose.

Abby was just winding up for the punchline of her advice. "I'm just saying be sure, sweetie. Be very sure of what you feel before you do anything. I think he's one hell of a special man, but I think both of you could really, really be hurt...unless you are absolutely positive of your feelings for him."

Paige opened her eyes. For some reason, her pulse was clattering at a thousand miles an hour...matching the mental wheels clicking in her mind. There was nothing odd about her sister's voice, nothing unusual about Abby being intuitive, but it did seem downright amazing that her sister was raising every exact fear she'd privately worried about herself. Amazing to the point of miraculous.

Stefan, of course, had the chance to talk alone with her sister earlier.

Paige stared hard into the darkness. She couldn't get it off her mind—his motivation for showing her those papers, his reason for feeding her sister all those fears and concerns. Like when she was carving a cameo, it seemed the answers and real truth were under the surface. Where only she could find them—if she were honest with her heart.

As soon as her sister left the next day, Paige hiked across the road to return his mountain of files. She had no trouble getting into Stefan's house—he'd left his back door unlocked—but he was gone. There was no sign he'd even been there that morning except for a coffee mug in the sink.

She'd just catch him later, she thought, which would work out better because she really wanted to take a trek into town. Only when she returned at noon with a mountain of parcels and an exhausted Visa, Stefan still wasn't back.

He never came home on Tuesday at all.

Or Wednesday.

By Thursday, she'd paced a flat spot on the carpet in front of her living room window. She'd tried working; she'd tried eating; she'd have tried chants and charms if superstitions would just make the lights pop on in his house. There was no chance of her concentrating on anything—but him. Stefan had never, even for an afternoon, just *disappeared* on her without a word.

Anything could have happened to him. He was a hopeless idealist who gave freely and openly from his heart. She'd never met a more vulnerable man than that damn Russian. Anyone could hurt him.

Worse yet, she was afraid she had. Badly. Maybe irreparably. Her worst fear had always been of hurting someone through her own bungling insensitivity, and the thought kept stabbing through her mind that maybe he'd tired of hearing doubts from her. Maybe he'd given up on her. Maybe he'd taken off for the sheer relief of getting away from her.

Sooner or later, she kept promising herself that he *had* to come back, if only to reclaim all his stuff. But the morning dragged into the afternoon, then slowpoked into the evening and still his car hadn't appeared across the street. By nine o'clock, it was coalblack and sleeting rain outside, and she finally gave up hoping for his return that night.

After switching off the downstairs lights, she climbed the stairs and ran a long, hot bath. She was submersed to the neck when she heard the muffled sound of pounding below. Pounding—and then an insistent doorbell. Then more pounding.

It wasn't as though she was napping—she surged out of the tub—but she still barely had time to stand up and reach for a towel before she heard Stefan bellowing from the foot of the stairs. "Are you up there, lambchop?"

Odd, how her heart stopped. Odder yet, it seemed too scared to start up again. Her chest felt as if a fist had squeezed panic-tight around her heart and just wouldn't let go. Possibly she'd been that afraid of never hearing his voice again, of never hearing him call her lambchop.

Or possibly her heart recognized exactly that this was it. Her one chance to take the biggest risk she'd ever taken. The one she'd been terrified to take all her life... and still counting.

"Paige? You there? Lambch—?"

Initially her voice emerged as a squeak, but it gained some volume on a second try. "I'm here! And I'll be down in two seconds! Don't you go *anywhere*, Michaelovich! Just sit down right exactly where you are!"

Stefan sat exactly where he was. On the stairs. Holding a velvet sack that he shifted from palm to palm as if he were weighing it. Waiting.

He waited more than two seconds. More than two minutes. When five minutes passed, though, he ran out of patience and lurched to his feet.

He'd just twisted around and intended to bound up the stairs when he saw the vision appear at the top. The vision had bare feet, a bare throat and was wearing a long nightgown in scarlet silk. Nothing more than two skinny straps holding up the whole thing, and the slinky fabric faithfully outlined every ripe, voluptuous dip and curve. She'd brushed her hair simply back from her forehead, no style, no artifice, but it flowed down her shoulders in a lustrous waterfall. The vision had her chin up, her shoulders straight and proud, a sensual woman reveling in her sensuality... but he couldn't help but notice the shine of panic in her eyes, or the vulnerable unsureness implied by her trembling fingers.

He'd learned a ton of American vocabulary, yet for several seconds, he couldn't seem to make his throat work long enough to push any of those words out.

He'd been prepared to track her down, to find her, to make her talk with him no matter what he had to do. He'd been prepared for reluctance. He'd been prepared for fears. He'd even come prepared with the offering in the velvet sack to bribe her into listening. But there was just no way, no how, he'd been prepared for this.

When more seconds of silence spilled past and he still failed to say anything, she either seemed to lose her nerve—or find it. Because she pelted down the stairs and launched herself into his arms.

He only had a micromoment to stash the velvet sack on the stairs. And then he reeled back from her jet-propelled launch...but he caught her. His fingers slid along the slippery silk at her waist, securing her steady. Her arms noosed around his neck, tight and hard, and her mouth slammed on his with the pressure of a bullet. The force was caused more by projectile momentum than actual passion, but the second kiss from her blew all the physics laws out of the water. So much for gravity. So much for the speed with which solid objects were supposed to fall.

As if she'd bathed in roses, her skin carried that feminine, fragile scent. She tasted warm and yearning, far softer than the silk-nothing she was wearing, far sweeter than spring. She was shivering from head to foot—no doubt from wearing that catch-her-death-of-cold outfit in the drafty hall—yet beneath that silk, her body was warm. Impossibly, vibrantly warm. The source of her trembling seemed to be vulnerability alone, and her kisses were perilously rich with the same emotion. His *lyubeesh* would seem to be offering him all the vulnerability of love, as freely as the wind and a thousand times more wild.

He kissed her back until their lungs both ran out of oxygen. Then he kissed her again, because he wanted to be very sure he was tasting hope instead of despair, and when he'd walked in that door, he'd never, never believed this huge a hope was even possible.

Eventually he pulled his mouth free. His hands, he discovered, had magically slid up all that wicked silk and tangled in her hair. They both just practiced breathing for a second, their lips only separated by inches, and her eyes, as liquid as dark sweet tea, locked on his.

"I'm getting the craziest feeling that there's a slight, remote chance you missed me," he murmured.

He hoped to coax a smile, but she was in no mood for humor just then. There was an ocean of anxiety in her eyes. "I missed you," she said fiercely. "I missed you for the past three days. And I missed you for the two weeks before that, when damn you, Stefan, you cooled down and made out like you were perfectly happy with us just being friends."

His shaggy eyebrows arched in question. "This was not what you wanted? To be just friends? You told me and told me—"

"I *know* what I told you. That we were wrong for each other. That your life was in too much upheaval and change to possibly be sure of how you felt about me. And dammit, you acted like you agreed...and you were a real *rat* for putting those citizenship papers in front of me. What did you think? That I'd fall for that horseradish about your using me to have a convenient American wife?"

"Horseradish?"

"Horseradish. As in bologna. As in ridiculous nonsense. You would *never* use a woman like that, Stefan."

She sounded sure—furiously sure—sure enough to insult him and loyally defend his honor at the same time. If she wasn't careful, his heart was going to take off and soar. "Da. This is true. But if I had to explain this—if it were a question in your mind—I had to believe you did not know me at all."

"I know you plenty, buster. Well enough to figure out that you put my sister up to having a talk with me. A big, hairy talk so she could raise every doubt and worry I'd ever had about you, about us."

"I liked your sister." He cleared his throat. "And possibly it occurred to us both that a little push was required to force your hand. You were swimming in doubts, my cookie. You were swimming in fears. To heap a little more on your head seemed the only way to make you confront these things. You are the only one who knew the truth of your heart."

She loosened the clasp on his neck. "You were never confused about your feelings for me."

"Da. This is also true. I beat to my own rhythm, which I admit is not always good. But I know what I feel for you. My life being in upheaval is a nuisance, but I am old friends with chaos. There is no relationship to my being unsure. I know my own heart."

"Well, I didn't know mine so easily." She swallowed, hard. "I wanted you to think well of me, Stefan. I wanted you to think I was...good. A woman worth respecting, worth caring for. I spent a ton of years feeling ashamed of the girl I'd been. It was so important to me to be in control of my feelings, my life, and especially my hormones. I haven't been in control of a hormone since I met you, *lyubeesh.*"

She'd called him lover in the Russian way, although he wasn't sure if she realized it. All he knew was that her lips were starting to curve in a smile. A soft promise of a smile, not a full-fledged one yet.

"You know what?" she asked him.

"What?"

"I don't have to be in control when I'm with you."

"You are just now coming to this conclusion?" He bent down, picked up the velvet sack and wrapped her fingers around it. She wasn't paying any attention. She was still looking straight into his eyes, even as he lifted her, hiking her long slim legs around his waist, and started climbing the stairs. He had no idea where her bedroom was, but he'd bet dollar for ruble he'd find it.

"I'm not ashamed when I'm with you." She didn't seem to notice or care where they were going. Or even that they were traveling at all. Her eyes were still talking to him. He might just fall into those liquid, dark beautiful eyes and never come out. "I was trying to be ruthlessly honest with myself, and somehow missed the truth. I love you, Stefan. I never felt ashamed of anything when I was with you. I love you so much my heart takes wings when we're together. So much that I feel like I'm more when I'm with you. I'm more than the woman I was, more of the woman I could and want to be."

He paused at the top of the stairs, and used an elbow to switch off the glaring hall light. Two other lights still spilled a yellow glow, one emanating from a bathroom. The other had to be her bedroom. It took him three seconds to figure that out. And four solid minutes to kiss her, right there, while her arms were laced around his neck and he was holding her, breathing her in as deeply as his own heartbeat. "Could I hear that part again about your loving me?"

"No. I have to warn you first what a bad bargain you're getting. I don't express my feelings as well as you, Stefan. That's nothing I can change overnight. I've been a stuffed shirt straight arrow too long. I'll have to work on the inhibitions—"

"I haven't noticed any particular problem with inhibitions when we are together, lambchop. But I wouldn't worry this too much. We could have an awful lot of fun working on this if any of them show up."

"I'm also a little on the absentminded side—"

"No kidding?"

"I can't balance a checkbook. Can't talk physics with you."

"More fatal flaws." He kissed her for each of them. And she exuberantly kissed him back, her eyes full of star shine now, and her skin flushed. Yet she pulled back—almost dislocating his spine—and her expression was suddenly serious again.

"I have a ton of real flaws, Stefan. But I also believe in loyalty the same way you do. There has to be something, someone, you can count on when the lights are out and life gets tough. I'll be there for you, love. We may not make a life by anyone else's rules, but we'll make a good life by our own. It just took me a while to figure out I had the right—the right to love you, the right to say it. The power to know I was strong enough to fight for you, with you, for a life together."

"Ah, Paige, you always had that power. It was always in you. You just had to believe in yourself." He sank back onto the four poster bed, with her collapsing intimately on top of him. Yet she frowned suddenly—as if just then realizing there was something hard and obtrusive between them. It wasn't him. She really hadn't seemed to notice until that moment that she'd been holding that velvet pouch. Now she looked questioningly at him. "Open it," he coaxed her.

The scarlet nightgown gaped enticingly when she raised up to get enough leverage to untie the silken cords. Her face mirrored a quizzical expression as her fingers connected with something smooth and cool—and familiar. She pulled out the jade cameo, stared at it for a long moment... and then at him. "*This* is where you were for the past three days? You went after my cameo?"

"Yes. I drove to New York. I went to find Harry. A nice guy, your Harry, maybe a brilliant market man for you in the art world—but not too life-smart. He'd sold it. I came close to killing him, but not to worry. We parted friends—as soon as he tracked down the new owners so I could buy it back."

Stefan took a long breath. "I wanted it for you. To show you... this is always how I've seen you, my lambchop. Strong. Beautiful. An innocence in all the wonder you discover in life. A woman who delights and takes pride in her sensuality, who has love that shines from her, inside, outside, all over. When you carved away all the doubts and fears... this is you. This has always been you. You're the only one who didn't see it."

Her voice softened to a butter whisper. "*Ya tebya lyublu,* Stefan."

"And I love you back. For now. For tomorrow. For the birth of our children and the years we are in rocking chairs. I give you my love, my loyalty, my heart."

She set the cameo on the bedside table. And forgot it. Just then, she thought her Russian badly needed seducing. He had some hopelessly romantic ideals about her. She planned to live up to every one of them.

She knew this man she loved. Knew him well. He was stubborn and unpredictable and emotional, a man incapable of backing down from his values and ideals, the most vulnerable of loners. The only thing ever standing between him and loneliness was love.

It would take a strong, gutsy woman to protect such a man. It would take a powerful and enduring love.

She was that woman. She had that love. And starting this moment, this night, she was beginning a lifetime sharing the loyalty of that loving bond with the man of her heart.

*   *   *   *   *

*Look for BACHELOR MOTHER
the next book of Jennifer Greene's*
The Stanford Sisters *series, coming to you
later in 1996 from Silhouette Desire.*

In July, get to know the Fortune family....

Next month, don't miss the start of Fortune's Children, a fabulous new twelve-book series from Silhouette Books.

Meet the Fortunes—a family whose legacy is greater than riches. Because where there's a will...there's a wedding!

When Kate Fortune's plane crashes in the jungle, her family believes that she's dead. And when her will is read, they discover that Kate's plans for their lives are more interesting than they'd ever suspected.

Look for the first book, *Hired Husband*, by *New York Times* bestselling author **Rebecca Brandewyne**. PLUS, a stunning, perforated bookmark is affixed to *Hired Husband* (and selected other titles in the series), providing a convenient checklist for all twelve titles!

FREE
Keepsake
Bookmark

Launching in July wherever books are sold.

MILLION DOLLAR SWEEPSTAKES
AND EXTRA BONUS PRIZE DRAWING

No purchase necessary. To enter the sweepstakes, follow the directions published and complete and mail your Official Entry Form. If your Official Entry Form is missing, or you wish to obtain an additional one (limit: one Official Entry Form per request, one request per outer mailing envelope) send a separate, stamped, self-addressed #10 envelope (4 1/8" x 9 1/2") via first class mail to: Million Dollar Sweepstakes and Extra Bonus Prize Drawing Entry Form, P.O. Box 1867, Buffalo, NY 14269-1867. Request must be received no later than January 15, 1998. For eligibility into the sweepstakes, entries must be received no later than March 31, 1998. No liability is assumed for printing errors, lost, late, non-delivered or misdirected entries. Odds of winning are determined by the number of eligible entries distributed and received.

Sweepstakes open to residents of the U.S. (except Puerto Rico), Canada and Europe who are 18 years of age or older. All applicable laws and regulations apply. Sweepstakes offer void wherever prohibited by law. Values of all prizes are in U.S. currency. This sweepstakes is presented by Torstar Corp., its subsidiaries and affiliates, in conjunction with book, merchandise and/or product offerings. For a copy of the Official Rules governing this sweepstakes, send a self-addressed, stamped envelope (WA residents need not affix return postage) to: MILLION DOLLAR SWEEP-STAKES AND EXTRA BONUS PRIZE DRAWING Rules, P.O. Box 4470, Blair, NE 68009-4470, USA.

SWP-ME96

"Motherhood is full of love, laughter and sweet surprises. Silhouette's collection is every bit as much fun!"
—Bestselling author **Ann Major**

This May, treat yourself to...

WANTED:

MOTHER

Silhouette's annual tribute to motherhood takes a new twist in '96 as three sexy single men prepare for fatherhood—and saying "I Do!" This collection makes the perfect gift, not just for moms but for all romance fiction lovers! Written by these captivating authors:

Annette Broadrick
Ginna Gray
Raye Morgan

"The Mother's Day anthology from Silhouette is the highlight of any romance lover's spring!"
—Award-winning author **Dallas Schulze**

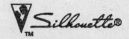

TM

MD96

SILHOUETTE®
Desire
CELEBRATION 1000

A treasured piece of romance could be yours!

During April, May and June as part of
Desire's Celebration 1000 you can enter to win an
original piece of art used on an actual Desire cover!

Or you could win one of 300 autographed Man of the
Month books!

See Official Sweepstakes Rules for more details.

To enter, complete an Official Entry Form or a 3"x5" card by hand printing
"Silhouette Desire Celebration 1000 Sweepstakes", your name and address, and
mail to: **In the U.S.:** Silhouette Desire Celebration 1000 Sweepstakes, P.O. Box
9069, Buffalo, N.Y. 14269-9069, or **In Canada:** Silhouette Desire Celebration 1000
Sweepstakes, P.O. Box 637, Fort Erie, Ontario L2A 5X3. Limit one entry per
envelope. Entries must be sent via first-class mail and be received no later than
6/30/96. No liability is assumed for lost, late or misdirected mail.

**Official Entry Form—Silhouette Desire Celebration 1000
Sweepstakes**

Name: _____

Address: _____

City: _____

State/Province: _____

Zip or Postal Code: _____

Favorite Desire Author: _____

Favorite Desire Book: _____

SWEEPS

SILHOUETTE DESIRE® "CELEBRATION 1000" SWEEPSTAKES
OFFICIAL RULES—NO PURCHASE NECESSARY

To enter, complete an Official Entry Form or a 3"x5" card by hand printing "Silhouette Desire Celebration 1000 Sweepstakes," your name and address, and mail it to: In the U.S.: Silhouette Desire Celebration 1000 Sweepstakes, P.O. Box 9069, Buffalo, NY 14269-9069, or in Canada: Silhouette Desire Celebration 1000 Sweepstakes, P.O. Box 637, Fort Erie, Ontario L2A 5X3. Limit one entry per envelope. Entries must be sent via first-class mail and be received no later than 6/30/96. No liability is assumed for lost, late or misdirected mail.

Prizes: Grand Prize—an original painting (approximate value $1500 U.S.);300 Runner-up Prizes—an autographed Silhouette Desire® Book (approximate value $3.50 U.S./$3.99 CAN. each). Winners will be selected in a random drawing (to be conducted no later than 9/30/96) from among all eligible entries received by D.L. Blair, Inc., an independent judging organization whose decision is final.

Sweepstakes offer is open only to residents of the U.S. (except Puerto Rico) and Canada who are 18 years of age or older, except employees and immediate family members of Harlequin Enterprises Ltd., their affiliates, subsidiaries, and all agencies, entities and persons connected with the use, marketing or conduct of this sweepstakes. All federal, state, provincial, municipal and local laws apply. Offer void where prohibited by law. Taxes and/or duties are the sole responsibility of the winners. Any litigation within the province of Quebec respecting the conduct and awarding of prizes may be submitted to the Regie des alcools des courses et des jeux. All prizes will be awarded; winners will be notified by mail. No substitution for prizes is permitted. Odds of winning are dependent upon the number of eligible entries received.

Grand Prize winner must sign and return an Affidavit of Eligibility within 30 days of notification. In the event of noncompliance within this time period, prize may be awarded to an alternate winner. Any prize or prize notification returned as undeliverable may result in the awarding of that prize to an alternate winner. By acceptance of their prize, winners consent to the use of their names, photographs or likenesses for purposes of advertising, trade and promotion on behalf of Harlequin Enterprises Ltd., without further compensation unless prohibited by law. In order to win a prize, residents of Canada will be required to correctly answer a time-limited arithmetical skill-testing question administered by mail.

For a list of winners (available after October 31, 1996) send a separate self-addressed stamped envelope to: Silhouette Desire Celebration 1000 Sweepstakes Winners, P.O. Box 4200, Blair, NE 68009-4200.

This July, watch for the delivery of...

An exciting new miniseries that appears in a different Silhouette series each month. It's about love, marriage—and Daddy's unexpected need for a baby carriage!

Daddy Knows Last unites five of your favorite authors as they weave five connected stories about baby fever in New Hope, Texas.

- **THE BABY NOTION** by Dixie Browning
  (SD#1011, 7/96)

- **BABY IN A BASKET** by Helen R. Myers
  (SR#1169, 8/96)

- **MARRIED...WITH TWINS!**
  by Jennifer Mikels
  (SSE#1054, 9/96)

- **HOW TO HOOK A HUSBAND (AND A BABY)**
  by Carolyn Zane
  (YT#29, 10/96)

- **DISCOVERED: DADDY** by Marilyn Pappano
  (IM#746, 11/96)

Daddy Knows Last arrives in July...only from

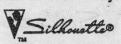

DKLT

You're About to Become a

Privileged Woman

Reap the rewards of fabulous free gifts and benefits with proofs-of-purchase from Silhouette and Harlequin books

Pages & Privileges™

It's our way of thanking you for buying our books at your favorite retail stores.

**Harlequin and Silhouette—
the most privileged readers in the world!**

For more information about Harlequin and Silhouette's PAGES & PRIVILEGES program call the Pages & Privileges Benefits Desk: 1-503-794-2499

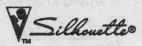

Silhouette®

SD-PP131